EVERYONE HAS A STORY

EVERYONE HAS A STORY

SAVI SHARMA

w

westland publications ltd

61, II Floor, Silverline Building, Alapakkam Main Road, Maduravoyal, Chennai 600095

93, I Floor, Sham Lal Road, Daryaganj, New Delhi 110002

First published by westland ltd 2016

This edition published by westland publications ltd 2017

Copyright © Savi Sharma 2015

15 14 13 12 11 10 9

ISBN: 978-93-86036-75-9

Designed by SÜRYA, New Delhi

Printed at Thomson Press (India) Ltd.

Savi Sharma asserts the moral right to be identified as the author of this work.

This novel is entirely a work of fiction. The names, characters and incidents portrayed in it are the product of the author's imagination. Any resemblance to actual persons, living or dead, or events or localities is entirely coincidental.

Due care and diligence has been taken while editing and printing the book. Neither the author, publisher nor the printer of the book hold any responsibility for any mistake that may have crept in inadvertently. Westland Publications Ltd, the Publisher and the printers will be free from any liability for damages and losses of any nature arising from or related to the content. All disputes are subject to the jurisdiction of competent courts in Chennai.

Dedicated to:

YOU

Everyone has a story to tell. Everyone is a writer. Some are written in the books, and some are confined to hearts.

Prologue

I was never a writer and I don't aspire to be one either. I was never a good reader and I don't know if I will ever be one. But now, I have been much more.

Every day, I woke up; I tried to find reasons to live. Every night, when I slept, I tried to find reasons to not die. Every moment, I tried to find reasons to hope, dream and love. But I never found them. Until I met you.

I saw chaos, confusion, and fear all around me. But not within me, after I met you.

Time decides our fate, our journey. And when time changes, everything changes. Everything. Sometimes for worse, sometimes for better. And sometimes, for the best. I never believed that. Until you happened to me.

It's not a story and maybe it's not love. It's about something more real than stories and more powerful than love. It's about you. Yes, you. Real and powerful.

I have never been happy with *someone*. I wanted to be with different people at different places with different feelings. I wanted to explore everything, know everyone. But then I explored you. And I found you are not just ONE, you are an infinity. An infinity of love, care, trust, respect, understanding. A universe of inspirations, aspirations, hope and happiness. Maybe you are the universe out there which I explore. Or the universe in me that I seek.

You do not start, nor do you ever end. You are constant, yet ever changing. You are everywhere and yet just with me. You are my creator or my creation, I question myself.

MEERA

1

WHAT'S YOUR STORY?

I had always been inspired by storytellers. I loved my job as an HR manager. It allowed me to interact with different people from different places, each one having their own different stories, bringing their own songs to the dance.

Life was a chaotic struggle, trying to search for where I belonged and who I was supposed to be. Each person I had interviewed had his or her own fascinating story, which made me wonder: what's my story? I didn't want to be 'normal', just like so many people I had met in life. Being only twenty-six, I wasn't exactly sure what the meaning of my life would really be, and where I could find it.

Every weekend I found myself sitting and listening to amazing authors at the café Coffee & Us. I was drawn to authors, fascinated by their ability to create other people's stories. How could they draw the truth from each individual and build a beautifully woven tale? I guess, having stories stuck in my own soul was the reason I needed to hear other people's stories. But I didn't just want to hear stories; my heart was aching to tell a beautiful story which would change people's lives, or at least mine.

So there I was at Coffee & Us, my hands wrapped around a warm, soothing cup of coffee. I could listen to the world around me, hear the songs of life, or I could put my earplugs in and mute out the world. I had seen so many writers come through these doors, and often I wondered if this café had some magic within its walls.

Kabir, the manager, paused in his duties and addressed me. 'When are you going to stop dreaming about being an author, Meera, and finally write a book?'

His voice might have sounded stern to an outsider, but Kabir had become my good friend. I'm not sure when, but at some point while I was becoming a regular visitor to his café, our casual interactions had blossomed into a warm friendship. He respected my opinions, and I treasured his.

'I don't know,' I said, frowning.

I ran my fingers through my long hair and let out a frustrated sigh, looking around at all the people in the small café. 'I think I will know when it is the right story to write. I just haven't come across it yet. I'm still searching for that unique story, the one that will inspire me to take that next step.'

He strolled to the counter where another cup of my favourite coffee—a frothy cappuccino—was placed. Kabir set it in front of me, smiling gently. 'I am sure, one day, I will be here, pouring coffee and fetching people their orders, as I listen to you up there. The place is going to be packed; you will see.' He smiled at the thought and I wondered for a moment if this was my dream or his. Of course, as friends, even our dreams would work in unison, wouldn't they?

Still, I lacked the confidence he seemed to have in my future success. As much as I wanted to take that next step to give my words the life they deserved, something held me back. I glanced over at the small area where so many writers had stood, taking a small sip of their ice water and clearing their throats before speaking the words I craved to say.

'I don't think I would be good enough to stand up there and face the world and a group of readers. It must take a lot of courage for them to do what they do,' I said, blowing on my coffee before taking a tentative sip. I smiled as the frothy bubbles clung to my lip and licked them off delicately. 'What if someone laughed at what I wrote?'

My friend chuckled. 'They would only laugh if you were reading something funny,' he said confidently. 'Now, tell me, are you coming for the authors' meet next weekend?' he asked.

'Definitely,' I said.

What would the weekend bring for me? Would I still be lost in search of my story?

~

'Live life in moments, not in days or years or your schedules. It's our misconception—most of the time—that we live our lives the way we want. Every single step that we take is influenced by others. Only the part that we hide from everyone else and keep deep within our heart, is our own. I strongly urge you all to realize that hidden part of yours. Go, live that part. Live your life. Don't let your dreams die within you. Trust me, your struggle, your fight, will be worth the risk in opening yourself up. Get up. Inhale the air of passion. Start your journey. Grab your dreams. Enjoy your mistakes. Dance to the rhythm of your heartbeats. Smile. Laugh. Love. Live.'

Author Arjun Mehra uttered these final words with confidence. His hands were clasped together as he looked expectantly around the café. His eyes met mine, and I felt my heart beat a little faster. It was as if he was speaking directly to me. But, in fact, he had touched the hearts of every single person in the café with his mesmerizing words. How was it that an author could hold such a magical power over people? I closed my eyes and imagined that I was the speaker, standing confidently in front of an audience. I smiled softly to myself. Perhaps one day I would actually be able to move a crowd like this.

'What's your story, young girl?' I was torn away from my thoughts when I realized Mr. Mehra was pointing directly at me. His soft brown eyes were holding mine, kindly, but with a challenging glint. 'What is your purpose in life?' He softened his question with a smile and, suddenly, it felt like a friend was speaking to me.

I took a deep breath. 'I … I want to write like you,' I began nervously, twisting the napkin in my hands as I decided to answer him as truthfully as I could. 'But I don't know what to write. I am inspired by the world around me, but I am still in search of a story that can change the lives of people.' My words sounded hesitant to my ears and I wished I hadn't spoken them.

Mr. Mehra nodded firmly. 'People need stories. Stories of love, hope, survival, wisdom and sometimes pain. Maybe you don't tell them the full truth; maybe you tell them lies. But what is this world? A lie in itself.' I was still held by his gaze, but I absorbed his words and heard others around me chuckle. 'But your lies are good lies. They change people and mostly for the better. I wish you the best,' he said warmly.

'Thank you,' I managed to say, shivering a little at his words, even though the café was almost uncomfortably hot.

'You are most welcome.' With that, he started looking for someone else to ask his next question. He turned his attention to a young man behind me. 'Sir, what do you do for work? What's your story?'

I had been so engrossed in his words that I hadn't noticed the man earlier. I turned around to see who he was speaking to and found a smart, handsome guy around my age. His black casual blazer suited his brown eyes and short dark hair and there was an air of confidence about him as he sat straight in his chair. I was surprised that I hadn't noticed him before.

'I work as the assistant branch manager at Citibank,' the young man answered. His voice was deep and rich.

Mr. Mehra continued his questions. 'What is it that you demand from life? Is it the thought of success, money or fame that brings you true happiness?' I found myself leaning toward the man behind me, curious to hear how he would answer.

The man cleared his throat. 'I have money, status and success, but I am still not sure what my purpose really is. I do know that there are days I want to escape the life I am living and grab my bags and just travel.' He trailed off and it seemed like his mind was already on those journeys.

The writer pressed him. 'What do you think you will find when you travel?'

'There will be no one who will follow me around, demanding things from me,' he responded. 'There will be no one pressuring me to meet deadlines. Money comes with a price, and for me, the price is both freedom and a real life. I hope someday I can make up my mind to chase my dreams.' The young man sipped his black coffee as he completed his answer. I saw his shoulders relax a little as he savoured the dark blend.

Mr. Mehra nodded his understanding before he swept his eyes over the audience once more. Holding up his hand, he said loudly, 'I hope the same for all of you here. Go ahead and make your dreams come true.' As his last words were spoken, concluding the event, the café filled with loud applause. I joined in, clapping so loudly, my hands began to tingle.

I had come to hear the writer, but I'd found myself deeply impressed, inspired and intrigued by the young man's answer. I wanted to learn more about him.

It was a bold move, and I took a deep breath before turning around to speak with him. But his chair was empty, a half-filled coffee cup sat on the table. I stood up, my eyes searching the room for his dark suit, and I spotted him leaving the café.

'I will see you next time,' I muttered, determined. He might have escaped for the moment, but the excited pounding of my heart told me that I had found my story.

2

MR. TRAVELLER

I was writing furiously in my notebook and barely noticed Kabir approach until he slid my coffee toward me. 'So you finally found a story to write!' he exclaimed with a happy grin.

I returned his warm smile and responded with a hint of excitement in my own voice. 'Well, yes. At least, I have a start.'

He slid into the comfortable red chair across from me. 'That's great. Tell me what you are writing.'

I shrugged my shoulders, suddenly shy. How could I give him a synopsis when I barely knew where my mind was taking my fingers? I sighed. 'It's about a traveller.'

'Interesting,' Kabir responded. 'May I read what you have written so far?'

Tilting my head to the side in deep thought, I responded honestly, 'I am not sure if it's worth a read.'

My friend narrowed his eyes at me and ran his hand over his head. 'You never know! Come on, now show me.'

'Okay.' I turned the notebook around to let him read my precious words.

I gulped. I hadn't been expecting him to read it out loud.

'I want to travel, travel the whole world. I want to go on a road trip. Stop at random places and explore their beauty. Run through the woods chasing a butterfly. Talk to new people with different cultures and different lifestyles. Listen to their stories; sit on a park bench in the sun. Enjoy every sunrise and sunset, sometimes from a hilltop and sometimes behind the trees. I want to spend hours beside a rushing river, feeling the wind in my hair and listening to the secrets hidden in the waves. Write a poem about the coldest, cloud-bound mountains and all five oceans. I want to cross my boundaries. I want to admire nature, and wonder at the magic of its creation. I want to make memories. I want to feel alive. I want to feel the Creator. I want to feel myself.'

His hand moved and I watched him turn the page. He read silently for a moment and I waited anxiously for him to continue. My heart was pounding, almost painfully.

'Life is not meant to be caged in your hometown, but it should be a wondrous place to be explored. I must explore all the nooks and crannies of this world. It has been a long-time dream of mine and, as I set out to do this, I realize that this

must be what it feels like to be a baby bird, perched on the edge of its nest, ready and anxious to fly to other places. I sometimes pity humans for not being able to migrate the same way animals can. There are no boundaries for animals, except what they are incapable of doing for themselves. Humans seem to be the only creatures who say they live freely, but they are bound by the restrictions they place for themselves. We are not just bound to our work, but to our homes. We do not roam. We live in a small, isolated location—a cage would perhaps best describe it. We have an area for business and we have an area where we eat the same foods and meet the same types of people. Pune has turned into that cage for me. I know everything there is about Pune, but like a lion in the zoo, I crave the freedom of standing on a rock and looking down at the kingdom below me. I want to see the birds flying, the elephants bathing happily in their watering hole and the gazelles running freely. That is the freedom which humankind was granted, and I am about to capture it by chasing my dreams across the horizon.'

Kabir's voice drifted off and he sat in silence. Trying to be patient, I traced my fingers over the rim of my coffee cup, then down the side, catching a random drop. Absently, I lifted my finger to my lips and licked it.

Still, he said nothing. Finally, I nearly yelled the question. 'What do you think?' I asked with a mixture of excitement and dread. 'How is it?'

He broke into a huge smile. 'It's lovely, Meera! I think it will touch millions of hearts,' Kabir said enthusiastically.

'Truly?'

He nodded and I let out a nervous laugh. 'Thank you!'

Kabir turned my diary back around, patting it happily. 'I would love to read more when you continue your story! I am sure as the story unfolds it will be even greater. Promise yourself one thing: never stop writing, Meera!' My friend stood, straightened the creases in his pants, and went back to work.

I stared at the words on the pages, fisting my hands in silent triumph over the pen. I was just happy to know he liked it.

Before I could start to write again, a young girl with the brown café apron walked over to me and handed me a folded napkin. I looked at her questioningly and, silently, she signalled for me to open it.

Curious, but confused, I lay the pen down and unfolded the napkin. It had just one word written on it in big capital letters: BEAUTIFUL.

I looked up at the girl. 'Who wrote this?' I asked. She turned back and pointed to a chair a few tables away. But there was no one.

'I don't understand,' I said.

She frowned for a moment, but then her face eased into a

smile. With a nod toward the café exit, she said, 'That young man said to give it to you.'

It was the traveller. He had escaped again.

~

I watched the man walk away through the dusty window before I noticed Kabir was looking, too. I stood up and rushed over to the counter. 'Who was he?' I asked Kabir.

'He is the assistant branch manager at Citibank on Telak Road,' Kabir said helpfully. 'He's been here several times since last month.'

I bit my lip in thought. 'Last weekend he was at the authors' meet as well. Has he told you his name?'

My friend shook his head and absently cleaned the counter between us. 'He doesn't talk much. However, I do know his name because he pays by credit card every time. His name is Vivaan.'

'Vivaan,' I repeated, tasting the name on my tongue. 'When does he usually come to the café?'

Kabir shrugged. 'Oh, when I say he is regular, he comes in often, but there is no fixed time. He drops by anytime he feels like it.'

I thought for a minute. 'Do you think you could text me the next time he drops by?' I asked.

'Sure,' Kabir said. 'But why are you asking so much about Vivaan?'

'He is the traveller about whom I am writing the story,' I answered.

I couldn't help but grin as I left the café with Kabir standing there, his mouth open in shock.

VIVAAN

3

TWIN DIMPLES

I stumbled over a small rock on the road as I walked up to my office. My mind was definitely not on the office building I was walking into. In fact, I almost resented having to go to work at all.

That was unlike me. Yes, I wanted to be free to travel, but I tried to make the most of where I was. Life had dealt me some rough blows, but I was always grateful for the constants in my life, my job being one of them.

My shoes squeaked on the polished floor, announcing my arrival before I could even get to my office. I couldn't wait to get past the sterile entrance and escape to my own area, where my shoes wouldn't make a sound.

'Sir,' the receptionist called after me. I groaned; so much for a quick escape. I turned to her, with what I hoped seemed like a genuine smile. It wasn't her fault that at this very moment, I hated my job. 'I have several messages for you. Your voice mail box is full again.'

Now, my smile was not faked. 'I'm sorry,' I said apologetically. 'I appreciate you taking the messages.'

'It's quite all right,' she said happily. I reached out and, as I took the slips of paper from her hand, her fingers brushed against mine. It occurred to me how attractive the receptionist was, but that was not where my interest was focused.

The woman crowding my mind was the young woman who had sat in front of me during Arjun Mehra's talk the other day, the same woman who was breathlessly talking to the café manager a short time ago.

I did not go back to the café seeking her out; at least, that's what I told myself. I merely wanted the best cup of coffee in the district.

But she was there when I arrived.

I was almost disappointed when she did not notice me, but after I sat down, I caught wisps of her conversation with Kabir.

I want to spend hours beside a rushing river, feeling the wind in my hair and listening to the secrets hidden in the waves.

It has been a long-time dream of mine and, as I set out to do this, I realize that this must be what it feels like to be a baby bird, perched on the edge of its nest, ready and anxious to fly to other places.

Kabir spoke the words, but in my mind, I heard

her voice echoing as the sentences replayed like a favourite song.

The words could have been written for me, I mused as I sat down in my soft leather chair, immediately pivoting to look out the window. *But that's foolish. She couldn't know my heart's desires.*

As she and Kabir had talked, I could hear the hesitation in her voice. She lacked the courage to present the talent that she possessed. I hoped she wouldn't give up; I could sense her writing was as much her dream as travelling was mine.

I blushed, thinking about the impulsive note I had left for her. BEAUTIFUL. It was meant to be taken one of two ways: her writing definitely had a deep beauty to it. But as spellbound as I was by her words, I was even more drawn to the girl.

She was petite, I laughed as I recalled, but amazing. The night she sat in front of me, I stared long and hard at her back, silently begging her to turn around. Her thin legs were tucked delicately under her chair, and I couldn't stop thinking about the soft brown skin that was too hidden by her flowing blue skirt.

But, mostly, I wanted to lose myself in her deep twin dimples and her dark eyes. Barely noticeable when she was concentrating, her brilliant smile brought multiple layers to her face. Like two angels were kissing her at the same time.

I shook my head to clear her image from my mind. I

vowed to go back the next day, to see if she had any reaction to the hastily-written note I'd asked the waitress to hand her.

I'd hurried away before; I would not hurry away a third time. I wanted to learn more about this blossoming writer in the café.

MEERA

4

MISS WRITER

Life throws unexpected turns at you. Only a few weeks before, I was looking for a story. And then, when I had one, I only had the smallest taste of what I knew could be a full tale. But I knew I had a story, and it would be the most touching story I had ever heard or written.

It was about six-thirty in the evening and I was about to leave the office. It had been a long day and my head ached. There seemed to be problems piled on top of other problems, and I had no solutions in sight.

My phone buzzed, but I was so tired, I nearly ignored it. I put my hand in my pocket, and then drew it out again, leaving my phone in its nest. A few steps forward and my hungry writer's curiosity was too much to ignore. Sliding my hand in the pocket a second time, I drew out the phone and tapped a few buttons. It was from Kabir. *'Your traveller is here.'*

I forgot my headache and started to rush to the exit as I tapped buttons furiously.

'Keep him engaged. I am coming.'

Moments later, I was on my way to the café.

~

I saw him through the window as I slowed my fast walk to a casual pace. I met Kabir's eye as I came in and I nodded my thanks.

I strolled to his table as I did a mental check of my clothing, my hair, and my makeup. Since I had worked through lunch, at least I knew I didn't have any embarrassing stains or pieces of food stuck between my teeth.

Taking a deep breath, I slid into the chair in front of him. 'So, Mr. Vivaan, how are you?' I gave him my most brilliant smile, as if we had planned this meeting for ages.

He looked up and blinked twice. 'Excuse me?' I could tell by his voice that he was astonished by my forward greeting. Or perhaps it was because I knew his name.

I crossed my legs and leaned back in my chair. My deliberate movements didn't betray my racing heart. 'I am sorry,' I began, 'but before you leave me for a third time, I think we should at least talk.' I turned to signal to Kabir to bring my cappuccino.

'Well, I never left you,' Vivaan said, looking deep in my eyes for the first time. For a moment, my calm movements began to falter. I could feel my hands begin to shake as he captured my gaze and refused to let it go.

I flexed my fingertips, silently commanding my hands to behave. I shook my head the same way my mother used to shake her head at me when I snuck away a chocolate cookie. 'But you never stayed. You escaped every time,' I replied with my eyes fixed on his. I felt myself discovering a new universe.

A frown creased his forehead. 'I love to travel. Don't you know that?'

'I know.' My voice was low, quiet. I didn't know what to say anymore. His eyes had cast some spell on me and I was completely mesmerized.

He spoke so softly, I could barely hear him. I absorbed his words by watching his full lips move as much as I heard the sound. 'And what makes you want me to stay?'

I wanted to stay in that universe for a very long time, that much I knew. And instinct told me that going soft would not hold him here. I cleared my throat, forcing attitude back into my voice. 'I love to write,' I responded. 'Maybe that's why.' I gave him a quick grin. 'Don't you know that?'

He smiled for the first time. It was one of those rarest smiles you encounter in your entire lifetime. The crystal hidden deep within a plain rock. These smiles have the power to change you from within.

'There is nothing to write about me,' Vivaan declared, and shook his head.

I plunked my hands on the table, lacing my fingers together. 'Everyone has a story to tell,' I insisted. 'Everyone is a writer. Some are written in books, and some are confined to hearts.' I was proud of my answer.

And there was silence for a few seconds. As we stared without blinking, I thought about the childhood game I used to play with my sister.

I felt, rather than saw, movement beside me and a cup was placed in front of me. 'Here is your coffee.'

I had no idea who supplied the cup, but I thanked her without breaking my gaze and delicately sipped my cappuccino, finally lowering my eyes.

I refused to speak next. It was his turn.

I counted three deep breaths before he finally spoke. 'You are good with words,' Vivaan said as he broke the silence.

'Thanks,' I said. 'And what are you good at?' I was eager to know more about Vivaan. He seemed so mysterious, and yet so wonderful.

Before I could get my answer, Vivaan's cell phone began to ring. He quickly reached down and checked the caller ID. His eyes were regretful when he looked up at me, disappointment rippling across his face.

Then he chuckled. 'I guess I am good at escaping,' he said.

Disappointment soared. 'Again?' I asked in a low voice.

'Always,' he whispered, leaning across the table so I could hear him.

'Why?' I prompted. I didn't want him to leave. I planned to keep him talking as long as I could.

He shrugged, the shoulders of his coat lifting nearly to his ears. 'Love.'

I wanted to cry, but there was a glint of teasing in his eyes. 'What?'

'I love to travel,' he explained. 'I can't stay in one place.'

Not yet, my mind called out. 'Will you meet me again?' I asked.

'Why?' he asked with a challenging tone.

I mimicked his tone. 'Maybe you are my story.'

'Miss Writer,' he said as he stood up. 'I am real, not fiction.' He laughed and started leaving.

I stood up as well and held his arm lightly. 'I am Meera,' I said sadly. 'Not Miss Writer.'

And before he could escape, I left the café first.

VIVAAN

5

A Late-Night Call

I sat on the edge of my bed, my hands draped over my knees as my mind raced from thought to thought.

I rolled my cell phone over and over in my hands, and then scrolled through my contacts until I found the one that I wanted.

She answered, her voice singing as she spoke my name. 'Vivaan! How are you, my love? It has been so long since I've heard from you!'

'I know,' I responded, shame running though my veins. 'I have been so busy with work...'

I heard her groan. 'Yes, work. Work is all you ever think about,' she said scornfully.

'That is not true,' I argued. But it was partially true. I carefully constructed my life so I was too busy for friends, family and thoughts.

Everyone wants to run away from one thing or another. At times, I want to run away from my own self.

'So,' she said, her voice brightening. 'Tell me what is going on. I want to hear all about what my darling nephew has been busy with.'

I knew I was forgiven. Priya Aunty never called me her darling nephew if she was mad at me. Oddly, I felt lighter with those few words. I thought fleetingly about how important words are, and how both the spoken and written word can harm … or heal.

'Well,' I began, turning my attention back to my aunt, 'you are right; I have been busy with work.'

'Work is boring,' she interrupted me before I could ramble on about loans and interest rates. 'It is necessary, but not a topic of conversation for today. What is fun in your world?'

I laughed. 'There is not much time for fun, Aunty.'

She would not give up. 'Have you been to the movies?'

'Not lately.'

'Any good restaurants?'

'Nope.' I heard her sigh in frustration. I could picture her sitting at her kitchen table, drumming her fingers impatiently. I grinned. 'I have been to a new café though,' I said.

'Really?' Her interest rose again. 'With friends?'

I laughed, knowing what she meant: friends of the female variety. 'No,' I said. 'They have a great French roast coffee that I love and the atmosphere is very fun. And they have writers coming in to speak...' I broke off, thinking of her. Meera. Her name to me was like a warm evening breeze.

'That sounds interesting,' she said. 'But you are still alone.'

'It is what I want, Aunty,' I said. 'You know I want to travel. I need to explore the world, see the Grand Canyon, the Great Wall of China.'

'The pyramids,' she offered, continuing my path of thinking. 'I know, Vivaan. And I know you would not have the opportunity to travel if—'

I broke in, anxious to cut off the rest of her sentence. 'But I can, and I will.'

'When?'

'I'm not sure,' I said. 'Perhaps soon.'

'Won't you get lonely?'

'Maybe,' I admitted. 'Maybe I will. But a person needs to learn how to be alone.'

'I do hope you find what you are looking for in the great, vast world you encounter,' she responded.

'And what would that be?' I teased.

'Only you know, Vivaan.'

MEERA

6

MR. LOVER

I decided not to visit the café for the next few days. A part of me was dying to go, but another part of me was still crushed by Vivaan's abrupt departure and I felt that I should stay away to heal my heart a little.

Not a single day had passed without my thinking about Vivaan. There was something about his mysterious persona that drew me towards him. I wanted to know more about him. I needed to know more about him. I needed this time to discover myself in someone else's story.

~

A few days later, I found myself wandering the gardens of Shaniwarwada. Growing up in Pune, this was one of my favourite places to visit. I loved walking around the fortification and its grounds, running my hands over the steel gates.

As a child, I used to look up at the spikes in the gates—put in place to protect the entryway—and wish for the time when I was an adult and able to reach them.

Why is it we are so anxious in our need to mature? It only opens us up for the possibility to get very, very hurt.

My phone vibrated as I was strolling down a stone walkway. I took it out of my pocket and looked at the sender. I didn't know the number. Curious, I read the message. *'Sorry.'*

'Who is this?' I texted back.

'Let's meet.' The sender didn't identify himself.

My heart fluttered. I had a feeling I knew who it was, but I wanted to be sure. A part of me was excited, but another part was slightly annoyed.

I ignored the message for a few minutes. Let him wait. Finally, I responded. *'Tell me who this is,'* I demanded.

'Don't you know me, Miss Writer?'

I was surprised by the fact that it truly was Vivaan. I wondered if he had got my number from Kabir after I left.

'I don't know you yet. You keep escaping,' was my reply.

'Then come and get to know me. Tomorrow, 7 p.m., Coffee & Us.'

I wasn't going to make this easy on him. I texted: *'I will handcuff you to the table so you cannot run.'*

~

One whole day seemed like an eternity, waiting and longing for the answers that Vivaan held in his mysterious persona. His story seemed to call me and intrigue me, beckoning me to unfold it slowly and write about it.

I intended to get to the café early, but by the time I finished getting ready, I was no longer early. In fact, I was thirty minutes late. The café was already packed and I glanced around everywhere, hoping Vivaan hadn't left. I looked over in the corner and saw him sitting as far away from the crowd as possible. He looked up from taking a sip of his coffee and smiled. Vivaan looked as good in casual clothing as he did in a suit and I ran my eyes over his jeans and black polo shirt as I made my way toward the table. Dark colours suited him well.

'I was starting to think you were never going to get here,' Vivaan joked as I sat down.

'Sorry for being late,' I said, but didn't offer any excuses. 'I am eager for you to tell me about yourself.'

'I will,' he promised, 'but first, how have you been since I saw you last?'

I forced myself to be patient. 'My work is going well,' I said briefly.

'Have you done anything fun?'

I smiled. 'Yes, I went to Shaniwarwada. I find a lot of peace in the gardens.'

'I love it there,' he said. 'So much history, so close to us.'

Then why do you want to travel? I was desperate to ask him, but I wanted to keep his focus on our table. I wanted his mind on me, in the coffee shop. Not roaming the world. 'Now, tell me about the mysterious Vivaan,' I demanded.

'I was born and brought up in Mumbai,' Vivaan started. 'I lost my mother when I was a child and my father raised me with lots of love and care.' I watched the pain flash in his eyes when he spoke of his mother, followed quickly by a wave of happiness when he mentioned his father. If emotions were colours, I know I would have witnessed a beautiful piece of artwork in a few seconds' time.

'I am so deeply sorry for the loss of your mother,' I said. My eyes started to fill with tears.

'It's okay,' Vivaan said as he quickly looked out the window, trying to focus on anything out there.

I was positive he missed her. I knew if I'd lost my mother at such an early age as he had, I would feel that a piece of me had been carved out, never to be replaced. Although he was still a stranger, a part of me wanted to hug him and comfort him.

I cleared my throat to bring his attention back to our table. 'Please go on and tell me more about yourself.'

He smiled. 'I completed my master's in finance and joined the banking sector. After a few years of hard work and a lot of struggling, I became the youngest assistant branch manager in our company,' he said proudly. 'I am probably going to be one of the youngest chief branch managers that the bank has within the next couple years.'

'Impressive,' I said truthfully. The man before me was certainly determined.

'That is all about me.'

I knew there was more that he held deeper and closer to his heart, and I wanted so badly to uncover his secrets.

I crossed my arms in a challenging position. 'That is the entire story you have about yourself?' I asked in disbelief, and I raised my eyebrows at him.

'Yes, that's my story.'

'Are you kidding me right now?' I asked.

'No, I told you my story wasn't that interesting,' Vivaan replied.

'I am not buying it for a minute! You have more to your story, and you are just hiding it! Tell me about your girlfriend,' I demanded, pushing further.

'Girlfriend? I don't have a girlfriend,' Vivaan said as he shook his head.

Wait. I wondered quickly if I had read him wrong. 'Then do you have a boyfriend?' I asked, suddenly puzzled.

'No! Shut up!' He laughed heartily. 'I don't have a boyfriend!'

'Vivaan,' I allowed my frustration to colour my voice. 'You drag me down here and you refuse to tell me anything!' I pointed out.

He sighed. 'Meera, I do not have a girlfriend. And, most definitely, not a boyfriend. I am single!'

I smiled my thanks as a waitress brought me my cappuccino before I turned back to Vivaan. 'Okay, what about your past? Did you have someone that you called your own?'

He sighed. 'I did have my fair share of flings, but there was nothing very serious. I am telling you the truth, Meera!'

I looked at him, confused. There must be more to him than this.

'I am disappointed.' I drew the words out the way my teachers used to when they chastised someone for not turning in a good paper.

'Why?' He frowned and began to tap his fingers against his coffee cup.

I explained patiently, 'I thought you would have some great love story to tell, something fascinating I could write about.'

'Meera, there are stories everywhere if you look.' I could hear the regret in his voice as he reached out, gently prying my fingers off my cup. He wrapped his hand around mine, squeezing gently, and I felt my pulse crackle at the friendly gesture.

'I don't find stories everywhere. The only time I found the one I wanted to explore, it was in your eyes,' I whispered.

Vivaan was silent. He signalled Kabir to bring another coffee.

When Kabir came up with a second round of coffee, Vivaan said, 'Maybe you should try to look somewhere else.'

'Where?'

'In Kabir's eyes.'

Kabir and I exchanged glances, and we both seemed equally shocked by Vivaan's statement. My second cappuccino sloshed in the cup as he put it on the table.

'What?' Kabir and I asked at the same time.

Vivaan laughed at our confusion. 'Didn't you ever notice how Kabir smiles when he looks at all the people who come in here? He doesn't care if they are young or old; he flashes a smile at them anyway.' I looked at Kabir, suddenly seeing my friend in a different way. 'The way he makes them feel here is like they are home, and we are all family.'

'That is something I try to do, yes,' Kabir said happily.

'He also makes the best coffee for his customers. I am sure he has been in love and that he has a story to tell,' Vivaan finished with excitement.

I sat there shocked at how he could pick up on every little detail a person had about them.

Slowly, I started to speak. 'I have to admit I have known Kabir a lot longer than I have known you. I know he is a lovely and courteous man and he serves his customers very well. But Kabir's love story never crossed my mind. Tell me, Kabir. Is Vivaan right?'

'Hmm…' Kabir stood there silently. His face coloured as he considered his words.

Vivaan reached over and pulled out a chair. 'Can you sit for a minute? I know it's busy in here,' he said.

Kabir's eyes looked over the place and then he nodded and perched on the edge of the chair.

'Tell us about yourself, Mr. Lover.'

7

COLD COFFEE

'Yes, I have been in love.' When Kabir began to speak, it was in such a sad voice I would not have recognized him if I wasn't looking at his face.

I was as surprised by his tone as by his admission. 'Who is she? What is her name? Where is she?' I couldn't stop myself questioning him.

'Her name is Nisha. She used to visit this café long before either of you two came here.'

'What happened? Why does she not come to this café any longer?' I asked.

Vivaan was silent, listening to Kabir through both his body language and his voice. I wasn't that disciplined; I was demanding, thirsty for the information. I wanted to know the story, and—as I got excited about it—itched to know the details. Kabir's story wasn't the love story I'd pictured him having, at least not in terms of causing the pain I could hear in his voice when he spoke of it.

'Meera, calm down! Let Kabir speak,' Vivaan said softly, flashing me a smile.

I nodded. 'Sorry Kabir,' I said in a quieter tone. 'I want to know everything about you and Nisha. Please go on.'

Kabir took a deep breath and looked down at his hands as he let out a sigh.

'I was brought up in a lower middle class family along with my younger sister. My father was a teacher in a government school, but he had to retire after he suffered a heart attack.'

'Oh,' I said quietly, but did not interrupt.

'Our savings went into his treatment. It was pretty hard for my family. My mother and younger sister both tried to do the household chores, feeding our family while managing his medical expenses. I decided to give up my college education and search for a job. My mother argued at first that she didn't want me to drop out of college, but I told her we didn't have much of a choice.'

He broke off, and Vivaan muttered, 'No, I can't imagine that you did.'

Kabir shook his head and continued. 'I immediately began looking for work, and fate brought me here. They needed a new person on their staff who spoke English well and, luckily, I was interviewed. It was by God's grace that I got this job.' He smiled happily. 'I became the manager in three years. Things have been good for my family since then, and every single day I thank God for the job He gave me.'

I had never known Kabir had it so rough. He was so friendly on the outside that I never guessed he held such sorrow in his heart. I wanted to scream 'Kabir, stop it!' because my eyes were already filled with tears. I deliberately bit my lip to keep from speaking.

'It was also because of your dedication and hard work,' Vivaan said.

'I never knew you went through such tough times. You never shared this with me. You are always so happy and smiling,' I pointed out.

Kabir sighed and shrugged his shoulders. 'You never asked me, Meera,' he said.

'What does this have to do with Nisha?' Vivaan asked, bringing the conversation back to Kabir's love.

Kabir's expression was distant as he began to recall the rest of the story.

~

After a few months of working here, I saw a beautiful young girl crying in the corner of the café. It made me quite sad that such a pretty girl was crying instead of smiling. I prepared a nice cold coffee with ice cream for her and placed it on her table. She looked up, stunned, and she wiped her tears. She said, 'I didn't order anything.'

I smiled and nodded. 'I know, but I thought maybe this will make you feel better.'

I could tell she was trying hard to smile as she thanked me. She came many more times after that. She was always alone, upset and distraught. Every day, I would do my best to try to make her feel better with different types of coffee, even though she didn't order anything. I never charged her. At the end of each day, her bill was deducted from my salary. It was then I realized that love makes you do crazy things.

One day, I finally gathered some courage to ask her about her sorrow. 'If I may ask, what happened?'

She looked shocked at my intrusion. 'None of your business,' she replied shortly. She stood up so quickly, she almost knocked the chair over. Then, she walked away. She stopped coming to the café after that.

~

'How come she was so rude? How could she just walk away?' Vivaan was annoyed.

'Look who is talking,' I responded, looking pointedly at him. He instantly realized what I meant.

'Did she come back again?' I asked.

'Yes, she did. My cold coffee brought her back,' Kabir smiled.

8

Kafe Kabir

Kabir's eyes glistened as if recalling a bittersweet time of his life. I pushed a glass of water that the waitress had left on the table towards him. He took a sip, and seemed to be collecting his thoughts before he continued narrating his story.

~

'May I have a cold coffee with ice cream?' a sweet voice said while I was busy making entries in the café register.

When I looked up, it was the girl for whom I had been waiting that past one month. There were no tears that day. She was wearing the most beautiful coral dress. She looked amazing.

'Yes. Sure, madam,' I stammered nervously.

'Nisha,' she smiled.

'Kabir,' I smiled back.

I prepared her coffee while she walked over to an

unoccupied table. She sat in her chair and kept looking at me. It was as if she had this hypnotizing spell she was holding over me—I couldn't understand why she was making me so nervous after a whole month.

'Thank you,' she said as I placed the coffee on her table.

'You are most welcome,' I said.

She took a dainty taste and smiled. Satisfied that she was content, I began to walk away when I heard her voice. 'I am sorry,' she said innocently.

I turned back to face her. 'Why?' I asked.

'For that day,' she said, gesturing for me to sit near her. There were only a handful of people in the café, so I could sit without feeling like I was abandoning my other customers.

I sat down and then shook my head, dismissing her apology. 'I should be thankful to you for all those days,' I said.

She put her hands on the table and leaned towards me. 'I need to explain,' she insisted. 'My boyfriend broke up with me and I was very depressed those days. I want to thank you for those coffees. They really made me feel better.'

'Thank you,' I said softly, though I felt something breaking inside me. 'I'm glad I could help in my small way.'

'You did,' she responded. 'More than you know.'

'Why did he break up with you?' I asked. It might have been rude to ask such a personal question, but I was puzzled that anyone would want to break up with her. She was beautiful beyond words or description. She had the face of an angel, and her hair seemed to frame it like a halo. Her eyes were large and I felt like she could search through my soul. Her lips were perfect in every way, as if she was a porcelain doll.

Nisha continued. 'We studied in the same college and became friends very quickly. He proposed to me within six months. I accepted. He loved me very much, I knew. He bought me a lot of gifts, and he seemed to care so much. We took our relationship to the next level after some time. We became very intimate and made love regularly. And then, one fateful day, I found out I was pregnant. He was scared and asked me to abort. I refused and asked him to marry me immediately. After all, he loved me, right?'

Tears were bright in her eyes. 'He said he wanted some time to think and would call me later. He never called me back and would ignore all my calls and messages. I was completely broken.' She couldn't control her tears anymore and started crying.

'Please don't cry,' I said, reaching out to hold her hands.

'I'm sorry,' she said, sniffing loudly.

I asked fearfully, 'Did you abort?'

'Yes. I had to. The day you asked me what happened to me was the morning of my abortion and I was very depressed.' Her voice was firm and I knew she was trying to act strong.

'I am sorry to hear that,' I said with tears in my eyes.

'It's okay. I am fine now. Thanks to you.'

I was surprised to hear that. 'Why me?'

'Not you. Actually, your coffees,' she laughed. 'Every day I would come here to sit alone and think about what I should do. I was on the verge of committing suicide. I had lost all hope. I no longer believed in love, life or anything good. But when you gave me different coffees every single day without me even asking you, I felt alive again. You showed me there were choices. Someone was there who genuinely cared how I felt without even knowing me. I knew there were bad people in the world, but now I also know that there are good people like you as well. Thanks for everything. You are the reason I look forward to moving on with my life,' Nisha explained with a smile.

'I am glad I made a difference in your life,' I said, a warmth filling my heart. 'I never knew such little acts of kindness could have such an impact on people's lives. But I wish you could have talked to me that day,' I said.

'What could you have done?' She was surprised.

'I could...' I stammered.

'What?'

'I could have saved your baby.'

She sat straighter in her chair.

'What do you mean? How?' Nisha asked.

'I would have married you,' I said, holding her hands.

She pulled her hands out of mine. 'What are you saying?' she asked angrily. 'Are you out of your mind? Why would you do that? Why would anyone do that?' Nisha was furious.

'Because I love you, Nisha. And love makes you do everything. Will you marry me?' I said, closing my eyes.

~

'Kabir! Did you really ask that?' Vivaan asked in disbelief.

He nodded, smiling. 'Yes, I did,' Kabir said calmly.

I wiped my tears as curiosity pushed away my sadness. 'Did you really mean that? Or was it just an impulsive thought?'

'Did she say yes?' Both Vivaan and I asked at the same time.

His eyes misted up. 'Yes, she did,' Kabir smiled.

I was so excited, I was almost vibrating in my chair. 'So when are you guys getting married?'

'I don't know,' he said. Disappointment was in his voice again. 'There is a problem.'

I groaned. 'After all this, what can be the problem now?' I was shocked.

Vivaan and I exchanged a look and he shrugged. 'Tell us,' he prompted. 'What is the problem?'

'She belongs to a rich family and I do not,' Kabir answered.

I was furious. 'Don't tell me that her parents refused to let her marry you.'

'No, they didn't. They agreed to the marriage and were actually quite happy about the idea.'

'Then what's wrong?' I asked.

Kabir sighed. 'I want to keep her very happy; I want to give her a secure future. I know money can't buy happiness, but the fact is, it's needed. I don't want my kids to grow up as I did. I want to earn a good living before I marry her.'

Vivaan nodded his understanding. 'But this is a steady job,' he began.

'It is a good job for a single person,' Kabir explained. 'But a family would struggle on my wages. Nisha is so used to a comfortable life. And, above all, I want to give my kids the best education and the lifestyle I couldn't afford.'

'True,' I admitted.

'Love is powerful,' Kabir continued. 'It can make you do things you could never imagine doing otherwise.'

Vivaan looked thoughtful. 'How do you plan to earn a more steady income?' he prompted.

'I want to start my own café,' Kabir responded. 'It had always been my dream, and now, it is more critical.'

'You would be so successful,' I sang. 'You do such an amazing job here, and if it was your own place, I bet everything you do now would be so much better there.'

'Thank you,' he said humbly. 'But it's not easy to just open up new doors. I need a lot of money and people to work for me. As much as I want to, I am very afraid I will never ever be able to start my café and marry Nisha. Right now, I am just trying to save as much as I can,' Kabir explained.

'How much money is needed?' Vivaan pressed further.

I wanted to cry once again. It was almost cruel to ask Kabir such things when it didn't seem to be something he could afford.

Kabir held up his hands. 'About fifteen to twenty lakh.'

Vivaan reached down to pick up his laptop bag and took out a cheque book. Kabir and I exchanged curious looks. What could he be doing? 'Here is a cheque for five lakh rupees.' Vivaan's voice took on a firm tone. 'Get started with it. The rest will be deposited soon in your bank account,' he smiled.

I was simply stunned and at a loss for words.

Kabir looked at the cheque in disbelief and shook his head slowly. 'But Vivaan, I can't take this. You don't even know me!' he cried out, pushing the cheque back to Vivaan. I watched several heads turn in our direction.

'Do I really not know you, Mr. Lover?' Vivaan dropped his voice so nobody else in the café could hear our conversation. He smiled and continued. 'And it's not a favour; it's a business deal. We will be partners on this. I will invest in the business and you will run the café. Do we have a deal?'

It didn't take long for Kabir to answer, although I could tell from his expression that his mind was racing in a million directions. 'Thank you so much.' Kabir was overwhelmed.

We were all silent for a moment.

'So have you thought of any names for your café?' I asked.

'I haven't really allowed myself to think that far ahead,' he admitted. 'Do you have any suggestions?'

'Kafe Kabir,' I suggested with a smile.

Kabir nodded and reached out to take our hands. 'We will do this together,' he said, determined.

~

What a day it has been, I thought as I pulled my favourite nightshirt on and climbed into bed. The sounds of Pune were already starting to dissolve as my mind began to drift.

This sudden change in our stories brought up a lot of questions inside of me. I wondered if we would really be able to start Kafe Kabir, but I also began to think about other things.

We all seemed to have a deeper perspective in life, we knew what we wanted to achieve, but were we really ready for that day when the change came? Kabir was afraid of change, and it was noticeable. He wanted to make his dreams come true, but he was unsure. Vivaan wanted to travel the world. I wasn't able to imagine not sitting in a café, drinking my coffee while speaking with him face to face. Without Vivaan, my comfortable surroundings would become very foreign.

Although I had my own dreams of being an author, it seemed as if reality had set in. Where would I fit in with everyone else, as they moved forward with their own lives? Would they forget about me ... or would I be too busy launching my novel to even remember them?

My thoughts were interrupted by a beep from my phone. I turned on my side and picked up my phone, smiling as I guessed who the message was from.

Sure enough, it was from Vivaan. *'Did you get your story?'*

'Yes. I did,' I replied quickly.

I curled my body around the phone as I waited for his response. *'What's the name of the story?'* he asked.

'Everyone has a story!' I texted back.

9

Two Packages

I arrived at the café to join Vivaan for a coffee after an exhausting day at the office. I had texted him earlier to let him know I would be late; I had some problems at work that I had to fix before I left for the day.

Vivaan was waiting for me at the counter. I saw him through the window and drank in the sight of him as I walked to the entrance. He was wearing a black business suit, set off nicely by a bright blue tie.

I rushed in with an apologetic look. 'I am so sorry I'm late.'

'It's okay. How was your day?' Vivaan said with a smile.

I groaned. 'I am completely tired and stressed out today,' I said as I flopped down in the chair next to him.

He looked sympathetic and stroked my arm before he broke into a smile. 'Well … I was thinking about you,' he began.

I grinned. 'You were?'

He nodded. 'I got you a couple things. I wanted to surprise you. It won't fix your terrible day, but it might make it a little better,' Vivaan said in a hopeful tone.

I blushed and smiled widely. 'You really got me a surprise?' I asked.

'Of course I did. I wanted something to put a smile back on your face,' Vivaan said, passing me a bouquet of flowers and two brown paper packages that were wrapped and tied with a bow.

I took the flowers and buried my nose in the petals, breathing in deeply. 'The flowers would have been enough for me to smile,' I pointed out.

'No, the flowers were just the beauty that I saw on the way here. The real gifts are in the packages. The flowers will soon wilt, but what is in these packages will always be with you.'

I was curious; I immediately set the flowers down and reached for the first package. I untied it to find an autographed copy of a book.

'This book is the one the author was discussing when we first met in this café. No matter where life takes us, I decided we should cherish that moment. It was the starting point to us becoming so close in friendship.'

Tears of happiness welled up in my eyes as I thought back to that night. 'Oh my, I am at loss for words,' I said, opening the cover to see what the author had written.

To my fellow author,

I hope I inspire you to be able to venture out on your journey as a writer. Your friend told me a lot about you and I cannot wait to be in a café some day, listening to you speak, as you did for me.

Remember that a great writer doesn't just put his heart into his book but his reader's heart too.

Best of luck,

Arjun Mehra

I threw my arms around Vivaan impulsively, hugging him. 'Wow, Vivaan! You really didn't have to do that! I don't even know what to say. I am so touched. So happy,' I said, my voice muffled in his shoulder.

'Oh no,' he said, settling me back on my chair. 'You can't say that yet. You have to open the other gift before you can say that.' Vivaan motioned to the other package that was still wrapped.

I quickly untied the second package to find a thick, sturdy book with a cloth cover. It had my name stamped on it. Confused, I opened the book.

'This book is to represent the fact that some day you will finish your novel and be the writer you want to be. I got you a blank one; and it is up to you to fill these pages with your story.'

I held the book to my chest, squeezing it as tightly as I had hugged Vivaan. 'Even if I write only my name in this, I want you to be the first person to read it,' I said. 'But, what is the occasion for such beautiful gifts?' I asked.

He shook his head and smiled. 'Nothing. Do we need occasions to celebrate life?'

I hugged him again. 'Thank you so very much for such thoughtful gifts!' I said as tears of happiness formed in my eyes.

It was hard to believe it wasn't that long ago we were complete strangers. He was yet a mystery and I was just a person attending authors' meets. We had come far in our daily conversations. We shared our views on life and relationships.

Every day, our friendship grew stronger. I could no longer imagine a time when Vivaan would not be sitting at the café, waiting to drink coffee with me, discussing the values of life and our thoughts about the world around us.

I wanted to dedicate my story to him. His gift would be a perfect place to write it in.

VIVAAN

10

SANDALS

As we met each day, we grew closer. I found myself thinking about Meera all the time. At work, I imagined her soft hair brushing my cheek, and remembered how warm she felt as she threw her arms around me that day in the café. No flowers could smell as fresh as this beautiful girl; no sunset could take my breath away as the look of adoration in her eyes.

If Meera wore her heart on her sleeve, so to speak, I held my own heart closely guarded. I wanted to open up more, but every time I started to take a step closer to that decision, I would think of the oceans I wanted to cross and the reasons why I wanted to escape. Freedom tempted me as much as the sweet girl in the café.

One evening, we met in the café. This time Meera arrived before I did and she turned around, flashing those deep dimples in her cheeks as soon as she saw me.

'Hi, partner,' Kabir called out a greeting as I walked in. By now the café knew his plans and it was no secret that he would be opening his own coffee shop.

'Hello, Kabir,' I greeted. 'Meera. How are you both today?'

As they responded, suddenly the press of customers became too much. Kabir turned to start preparing my coffee, but I stopped him.

'Another time, my friend,' I said. I saw the confusion in Meera's eyes as I broke away from our customary ritual.

I put some money on the counter for Meera's cappuccino and held out my hand to her in invitation.

'Are we going somewhere?' she asked. 'I don't understand.'

'Five days of rain, and it has finally stopped,' I said, gesturing to the windows. 'Let's go for a walk.'

Grinning, Meera stood up and gathered her coat and bag. 'That is a wonderful idea,' she said, excitement in her voice.

'The park is so close,' Kabir said helpfully. 'The benches will probably still be wet, but it would be a wonderful time for a walk.'

I looked at Meera. 'What do you think?' She nodded.

Kabir quickly poured the rest of Meera's cappuccino in a paper cup and snapped a lid on it. He handed me a steaming paper cup of my own. 'Enjoy, kids,' he said with sparkling eyes.

We stepped out into the air, clean and fresh-smelling. It was warm and a little humid. Meera had her long hair pulled back in a ponytail and I noticed the tendrils around her face curling softly in the humidity.

We turned and began walking in the direction of the park, careful to give way to the rushing pedestrians as we took a much more leisurely pace.

'Tell me about your day,' I invited, threading my fingers in hers. She looked surprised at the gesture, but didn't comment.

'It wasn't too bad,' she began. 'My boss is on vacation and even though I have more work, it is a relief that he is gone for a while.'

I chuckled. 'Does he make your life rough?' I asked.

Meera shrugged her shoulders. 'I don't think he means to be difficult,' she began. 'But he has a way of making everything seem like an emergency. Even the simplest tasks appear to be a crisis.'

'I've worked with people like that,' I responded. 'It does make your days longer when there seems to be a problem everywhere you look.'

'Imagine how miserable those people truly are on the inside,' she said. 'They must have ulcers from all the stress. Life is too short to worry about everything!'

We walked in silence, finally coming to the park. We waited for the lights to change to cross the street, and then darted across the busy roadway before the lights turned again.

At the edge of the park, Meera stopped suddenly. 'What's wrong?' I asked.

She looked down at her feet, and lifted a stylish high heel in explanation. 'I'm not exactly dressed for a walk,' she explained.

I slapped a hand to my forehead. 'Sorry, I didn't even think about that.'

She shook her head, dismissing my concerns. 'It's quite all right,' she said. 'I just need to make some adjustments.'

She reached out her hand, clamping it tightly on my arm, and reached to pull a sandal off. 'You're taking your sandals off?' I laughed.

She grinned and nodded. 'Can you hold it for a moment?'

I took the sandal and held out my arm while she teetered on her bare foot, pulling the other one off. Then, she placed both sandals in her large shoulder bag.

'Better?' I asked, amused.

She nodded firmly and we began walking again. I couldn't help it; she was even shorter than before and I gave in to the need to throw my arm around her shoulder. In response, she snuggled closer to me as she padded along on the sidewalk.

We walked through the park, enjoyed the evening as we chatted about some of our favourite childhood memories.

I loved making her laugh; the sweet sound filled my soul with such happiness, I couldn't imagine how I had navigated through my days before I met her.

When we left the park and returned to the street, Meera pulled her sandals out of her bag and tried to slip her feet back into them. While she was balancing on her first sandal, she wobbled directly into me.

'I'm sorry,' she laughed as I caught her, holding her firmly until she was steady in her sandals once more.

'It's quite all right,' I responded, still holding her tightly. I didn't want to let go.

Meera looked up at me expectantly as I reached out and twirled one of the curls near her face around my finger. 'I've been waiting to do that,' I admitted, my voice deep with emotions.

'You have?' she asked, her eyes locking with mine.

I couldn't talk any more. I brushed her soft cheek with my hand, running my finger over one of her precious dimples before I leaned down and kissed her.

MEERA

11

SCARED

After two months of hard work and dedication, we were nearly ready to see our dreams come true for our beloved friend. Kafe Kabir was inaugurated with a grand celebration and a 'Kabir Weds Nisha' declaration.

During that time, I had met Nisha and we instantly connected with each other. She had such a friendly nature and was so beautiful; I was not surprised that Kabir had fallen in love with her so quickly.

Kabir, Nisha, Vivaan and I became very close friends over those happy months. We met faithfully every weekend at Kafe Kabir and had a great time. Although both Kabir and Nisha were working hard to make the place a success, they were able to take time off to nurture our growing friendship. I valued those times together, just as much as I knew the other three did.

'I know I haven't known you as long as Kabir has, but

you have made him a changed man,' I said one evening to Nisha. 'He loves you so much! I often dream of finding the kind of love that you and Kabir share.' I thought of Vivaan. We were still waiting for him to arrive.

Nisha smiled and ran her hand down my arm. 'Meera, sweetheart, open your eyes. Even I can see that you love Vivaan. It is no big secret why you are pursuing him for your stories. Your heart has told you that you have finally found the person whom your soul loves and recognizes,' she said. 'It is scary, I know, to fall in love. But Vivaan is a good person and I think the two of you would be very happy.'

I knew she was right. I had deep feelings for Vivaan, but I had never said anything to him, apart from some small hints, even after the kiss we shared at the park.

'I wish I could express my feelings to him,' I whispered. It felt so good just to be able to say that to Nisha, but at the same time, the admission filled my blood with a biting cold fear.

'Why haven't you told him how you feel? It is obvious you are truly falling in love with him!' Kabir said, bringing my favourite coffee.

I shrugged. 'What if he doesn't feel the same way for me, Kabir? I am afraid he will reject me,' I said as my face turned red. It was embarrassing to tell my friend how I felt. But then again, he had told me and Vivaan about Nisha and look how well that turned out.

'Meera, if you love him, let him know how you feel,'

Kabir insisted. 'If you don't make an effort to tell him and he doesn't know how you truly feel, he might not ever know. You wouldn't want something like that to pass you by, do you?'

'No, Kabir, I don't want something like that to pass me by,' I replied as I saw Vivaan coming through the door.

~

My story had turned out to be quite intriguing and filled with events that I only dreamed about. A lot had changed since that first time I met Vivaan. Kabir's love story alone had changed me a lot. I was starting to long for the type of relationship he and Nisha shared. I wanted someone to share my happiness and my life with.

I had to gather the courage to tell Vivaan how I truly felt. My hands began to shake as I thought about revealing my feelings. What if he laughed? No, he would never do that. But what if he didn't feel the same way? I wasn't sure if I was brave enough to tell him I loved him.

But I didn't know if I had the courage to hold my feelings in any longer, either.

It was midnight when I picked up my phone and sent a message to Vivaan. *'I can't sleep. Are you still awake?'*

After few minutes, I received a poem from Vivaan.

'Not the people but the mind,
Not the storm but the silence,

Not the answer but the question,
Not the result but the reason,
I am scared of.

Not the real but the dream,
Not the moment but the memory,
Not the lie but the truth,
Not the death but the life,
I am scared of.

Not the end but the start,
Not the strangers but the known,
Not the hate but the love,
Not the world but the me,
I am scared of.'

I was not sure how to respond. Should I praise his beautiful poem or should I be worried that something was wrong with him? I replied, *'Let's meet tomorrow.'*

I slept, my hand wrapped around my phone, waiting for his reply.

12

No Goodbyes

The next day, when I woke up, I was surprised not to find any message from Vivaan. I figured he must have fallen asleep too, so I decided to call him.

'The number you are trying to call is switched off,' a tinny voice announced. 'Please try again later.'

Perhaps he forgot to pay his phone bill in all the excitement of getting Kafe Kabir up and running, I thought.

I showered and got dressed, sliding into a soft, long skirt that I knew Vivaan liked.

I tried to call him again, but got the same recording.

I wasn't sure what was going on. My mind went to the sad poem he had sent me the previous night. I kept calling, but his phone remained switched off.

Finally, I dialled Kabir's number.

'Hello,' he answered.

'Kabir, there is something wrong with Vivaan,' I began.

'He has not replied to my messages, and now, his phone is switched off.'

'He might be busy working. I am sure he will get back to you soon,' Kabir said, consoling me. 'Don't worry.'

'I hope he does,' I said, and hung up.

~

Two days went by and there was no message or call from Vivaan. Kabir grew more and more worried. In the meantime, I was becoming frantic.

We finally decided to go to Vivaan's bank and figure out the reason he wasn't responding. It didn't take us long to get into the car and arrive at Citibank.

I was unable to speak, so Kabir took over. 'Can we please talk to Vivaan?' he asked a teller.

She shook her head, allowing her long black hair to sway back and forth. 'I am sorry, Vivaan doesn't work here anymore. He resigned two days ago.'

The words hit me as if someone had punched me in the stomach and knocked the wind out of me. Vivaan had resigned from his job as the assistant manager at Citibank. He had not told me that he was going to resign.

'Do you know where he works now?' Kabir pressed nervously.

The teller shook her head again. 'I don't know where he went, but I doubt he decided to work anywhere else. I heard him telling the manager that he was leaving … no, he said he was "escaping". It seemed like he had had enough from life.'

I gasped and held on to Kabir as my knees threatened to buckle. I shook my head in disbelief. I couldn't believe he had made all these arrangements and hadn't told any of us. My body, my mind were numb when I realized he had truly 'escaped'. I had dialled his number so many times, but there was no response. There had been no goodbye or explanation from him.

I tried to be brave and at first I was determined to brush it off. This was Vivaan, and his dream was to escape. I knew that from the very first night I set my eyes on him. But there had never been any real hint that he was just going to get up one day and leave.

I couldn't help thinking, how long had he planned this? Had it always been his plan to vanish one day? He had told me several times that he couldn't stay long in one place due to his love for travelling. I knew that. Then why did it crush me when the day finally came that he fulfilled his dream? He had moved on. Without me.

We somehow managed to control our emotions and reached Kafe Kabir.

'Come on Meera, don't cry,' Kabir said as he noticed my eyes begin to fill up. 'Meera, we all knew that he loved to travel. But don't worry, he will be back.'

'He didn't even say goodbye,' I broke down, throwing

my arms on the counter and sobbing into them. I was heartbroken, and worse, I already missed him.

Kabir patted my shoulders. 'Oh Meera, stop your tears. I am begging you to stop, or I am going to start, too,' he said, his voice breaking.

I brought my head up and glared at him. 'How can you ask me to stop crying? My heart has been ripped out of my body! The day I finally get the strength and courage to tell him how I feel, he is gone. I am lost without him!' I threw my head back down and kept crying.

'Meera, we will all miss him and you have every right to miss him,' Kabir soothed. 'All we can do is stay busy and keep him in our hearts and memories until he returns.'

No matter how long his trip would be, it was a very long time to live without Vivaan in my life. His beautiful smile wouldn't be warming my soul any longer.

I sat at the counter as my whole world continued to shatter around me.

Kabir brought me my cappuccino. 'At least you have a book to write! You can keep yourself busy with that. Maybe you can finish your novel before he comes back. Wouldn't he be proud of you then?'

My whole body was still numb and I felt isolated in the crowded café. I knew there was still a lot more for me to do and accomplish in my life, but I thought Vivaan would be there to share it. Now I was trying hard to fit back into that place where I once belonged before he entered my life.

I finally realized that the walls of the café no longer had any miracles left within them. I had lost all interest in everything about my life or my story. Everything reminded me of Vivaan.

13

BLANK PAGES

It felt like it had been forever since Vivaan had been here. There were still times when a steaming black coffee would be served to the person next to me at the café, and I would turn to see if it was Vivaan.

Writing had become a struggle. Many times I would read what I had written and cry. I traced my fingers over the precious book with my name on it, trying to find the courage to turn to one more blank page.

It was only when I had lost Vivaan that I realized I loved him more than anything in this world. I would have given anything to get him back.

'Kabir asked me to come in and talk to you,' Nisha said one day. I jumped in my seat, not having heard her approach.

'Nisha, there is nothing you can do or say to bring back Vivaan,' I said sadly. 'I have to figure out how to get over this hump so I can finally finish this story though.'

She nodded her understanding. I watched as she signalled Kabir to bring her a cold coffee with ice cream.

She sighed. 'Life is about twists and turns,' she began. 'It is about experiencing everything and anything it throws your way. Some people are here to teach us lessons while other people will be here forever as we grow old together. I am not sure yet if Vivaan will be there for you, but time will heal your broken heart.'

'I'm sure it will,' I said, although I didn't really believe her words or mine.

Nisha pressed on. 'Just concentrate on everything you wanted. This is the time in which you can finally be an author. There is no one here to slow you down or stop you.'

'But what if I never see him again?' I finally voiced my greatest fear.

Nisha rubbed my arm lovingly. She was such a dear friend, and I thought of the heartaches she had experienced before Kabir proposed.

She was silent for a moment as she put her words together. 'I have heard that if two souls are destined to meet, the universe will always find a way to make the connection. Even when you lose all hope, certain bonds cannot be broken. They show us who we were, who we are and who we can become. Amidst everything, nature will always find a way.'

Despite her confident words and my brave determination

to move forward and keep writing, I wasn't sure how to move on without Vivaan; that was the truth. Vivaan might never have disclosed his full story, but he always told me just enough to keep me interested and wanting more.

There was something about Vivaan's story that had called my soul as if it was a piece of mine as well. It was hard enough that he had moved on, but having to finish a book where he was the main character and every thought I wrote was about him was even harder to deal with. Every page reflected his stories.

I thought about one conversation we'd had when I asked him where he wanted to go.

He explained, *'I want to travel but I don't mean I want to be a tourist. I want to be a traveller, an explorer. I want to explore another country and become part of it. Climb the hills, swim the rivers, walk on beaches, find the libraries, discover secrets and stories of the places.*

'I want to meet people who are different from me, but people with whom I can still be the same. I want to see things with new eyes and listen with new ears. I don't want to come home whole; instead, I want to leave a piece of me in each place I have been. And thus, it would be an even exchange, as I take a piece of each place I visit.'

Was that how my book would end? With Vivaan vanishing like he always did, without a trace or a word? I didn't want to end the book in such a way that made no sense to me. I didn't want it to end suddenly in tragedy and loss.

It was supposed to be the greatest story that anyone would ever know. At the moment, I was only writing the world's most incomplete story.

No one understood that, without him, my story was incomplete. Least of all, Vivaan.

I didn't say a word to anyone when I left the café. I didn't talk much now. My courage to go forward in life, the confidence to work towards everything I wanted to accomplish … all of it seemed to be locked away and hidden. I wasn't sure if it was still within me and just carefully hidden, or if Vivaan had taken my dreams with him as well.

I walked to my car and began driving. It was a route I had taken a thousand times to get to my apartment. The traffic was unbearable. The sun was beginning to set, and the burst of colours on the horizon made it look like flames were dancing in the sky. Beautiful shades of blue, pink and purple spread across above me.

'*I want to travel, travel the whole world. I want to go on a road trip. Enjoy every sunrise and sunset, sometimes from a hilltop and sometimes from behind the trees.*' Vivaan's voice echoed in my mind.

Tears began to form again as I hit the steering wheel with the palm of my hand.

As quickly as my anger bubbled up, it settled even more rapidly into a bland sadness. 'I hope you at least see this sunset, Vivaan, and you remember me here, where you left me,' I whispered quietly in my car.

VIVAAN

14

My Memoirs

The last three months had been crazy. Since I had left India, I had seen so much of the world.

I started my adventures in China. I felt the burn in my calves as I walked part of the Great Wall and tasted food so delicious that my mouth was watering weeks later remembering it. The blue waters of the Peacock Riverbed in Jiuzhai Valley reminded me of the skirt Meera wore the first night we met. I smiled at the memory and moved on to the waterfalls in the park, their thundering sound nearly too much for my own thoughts to bother me.

I went to Tokyo next. The parks they had were amazing; there were zoos as well as lakes on which people used paddle boats. I saw the sunrise from Mount Fiji and it was breathtaking. From my hotel, I walked to Yoyogi Park and later toured the Hamarikyu Gardens. It was such a busy city, and I was ready for a quieter stop next.

In Italy, I explored Mount Vesuvius, and later toured the ruins of Pompeii. It was humbling to stand in the excavated walkways of the ancient city and face Vesuvius. A shiver went down my back as I thought of the thousands that perished when the great volcano erupted.

I took a ferry tour around the Isle of Capri and remained frozen on the side of the ship as it circled the area. It was beautiful to see the island rising out of the ocean in front of me. I opted not to take the gondola ride to the top of the island, but enjoyed the scenery from below just as much.

I went to Alaska and, bundling against the cold that seeped into my very bones, I saw the aurora borealis. Shivering violently, I watched the haunting blues and greens of the northern lights dancing in the crisp air with only the snowy surface of the ground to reflect it. During the day, I saw animals and birds I could have never imagined existed. I was overwhelmed when I saw my first moose; there was something oddly adorable about the brown, long-legged animals, but their sheer size was awe-inspiring. I couldn't help but grin as one looked up from the bog where it was eating. The water draining from its mouth dripped off the vegetation that it was munching contentedly. I had focused my camera carefully, hoping to capture the awkward beauty of it.

I went to New York City because it is called the 'Gateway to the World'. The city was always busy, and it stayed open all night. Even in the early morning hours cars rush by and, during the day, people are in such a hurry that they forget how to live all together. It was so bright there, with all the city lights, that I could not see the stars. There were just dark skies, there was none of the beauty that I knew was hidden beyond the neon lights that formed a visual umbrella, lighting up and masking way too much.

A quick flight later, I was in front of another thunderous spill of water—Niagara Falls. I walked out on the Prospect Point Observation Tower. As dusk fell, I sat on the cold concrete and hungrily watched the multi-coloured lights illuminating the rushing water.

The next morning I donned a plastic blue poncho and took a ride on one of the small boats that skitter up Niagara River to the bottom of the falls.

I felt the powerful engines fighting the currents in the river as we inched up to the falls. The roar was deafening, but I couldn't hide a laugh of exhilaration as I felt the spray from the falls coating my face. The monsoons of India brought such a relief, but the force of the falls, with the light, insistent spray, was breathtaking. I watched several couples cuddling on the short voyage, their transparent blue hoods pressed together as they kissed or tried to make themselves heard over the roar.

I went to the Grand Canyon next. I wanted to see if it would be as beautiful as I expected it to be. Truly, any photo could not do justice to the view. It was awe-inspiring to see such an enormous cavern in the earth. I took a donkey ride to the bottom, loving each jostle as the donkey's nimble feet picked the way down the steep paths.

Returning to the top again, it was nearly sunset and the view took my breath away. It was as if a small child had found his mother's painting palette and mischievously splashed all the different shades across a canvas.

15

Emma

Back on the east coast, I decided to spend a few days in Boston. After NYC, I wasn't sure if I was ready for the press of people there, but I was drawn to the rich history of the area. It was one of America's birth cities, and I looked forward to learning a little more about the culture.

I decided to take the subway to Boston Common, a large park in the middle of town. The subway was very confusing, but I found some helpful college kids who helped me navigate through the different colours and lines. Still, I was happy to emerge from the subway as I stepped out onto Tremont Street, at the edge of the park.

There were people milling about, but it wasn't as overwhelming as New York had been. In fact, everyone seemed very friendly. There were college kids lounging on the sun-soaked grass, and people playing Frisbee. Walking by a playground, I stopped to watch an old man making balloon characters for kids and laughed when he handed me a green dog. As I was leaving, a little girl's balloon popped and she started wailing. I gave her my dog and was rewarded with a huge hug. I laughed. She smelled like apples.

'You have a pretty smile,' the little girl said innocently. 'Want to come to the pool with us?'

I looked at her father for help. My English is very good, but I had no idea what she was talking about. The father grinned. 'I think you have a new friend,' he offered. 'This is Emma,' he said, running his fingers through her damp, blonde curls. 'My name is Max.' He held out his hand.

'Vivaan,' I said.

Emma giggled. 'That's a funny name,' she said. 'And you talk funny!'

'Emma!' her father scolded.

'It's okay,' I said. 'I am from a different country, far, far away,' I explained to the little girl.

'Where is your little girl?' she asked.

'Emma!'

I smiled. I was enjoying this spirited little creature very much. 'I don't have a little girl yet. I hope she is just like you when I do, though!'

She started tugging her father's hand. 'I guess we're heading to the pool,' Max said apologetically. 'You are welcome to join us, though. It's so hot today, even I'm going to dip my feet!'

I agreed happily. After travelling for so long by myself, it was nice to have a little company again.

Emma slid her hand in mine and half-skipped, half-galloped as we made our way to the pool. It was actually a large stone area with a small fountain in the middle and only a few inches of water. Kids were scampering and splashing under the fountain. At the side of the pool, Emma dropped to the ground and yanked off her shoes, jumping in the water with a glorious splash.

Max and I followed her example. It was odd to be pulling off my shoes and socks in front of two strangers, but Max didn't seem to be bashful as he kicked off his sneakers.

We sat on the edge of the pool and dipped our feet as Emma played with her balloon dog in the water.

'Do you live here or are you visiting?' Max asked.

'I'm only visiting,' I replied. 'I wanted to see a little of the world so I quit my job in India and started to tour.'

'Wow,' he responded. 'How long will you be travelling?'

'I don't know,' I said. 'I would never go home but I will have to eventually. If travelling was free, they would never see me again.'

'They?' Max asked.

'My friends back in India,' I said.

'So, you're not married,' he responded.

'No,' I said. 'You?'

'Nope. Emma's mom and I split up soon after she was born. We realized we were better friends than spouses.'

'I'm sorry,' I said automatically.

'No, no. It's good for us. Of course, I don't see Emma as much as I would want, but the times we do have are precious. I cherish every second I have with her. So, there is nobody special you left behind?'

I thought of Meera. 'Yes, sort of,' I said, stretching my legs out and swirling my feet in the cool water. 'She's more like a friend, though.'

'But...' he pressed.

I shrugged. 'But there could be more,' I admitted. It felt good to finally admit that to someone, even if he was a complete stranger.

'Will she be there when you return, do you think?'

I sighed as I thought about it. 'I hope so.'

He reached over and patted me on the shoulder. 'Then, my friend, you might not want to take too much time to go back.'

16

KNOWN STRANGERS

Finally, I sat in the Promenade Plantéea Park in Paris with an evening picnic of crusty bread and Cantal cheese as I watched one of the most beautiful sunsets since I had begun my journey. It looked like the sun was bursting into the colours of fire and then fading into pinks, blues, and purples.

The couple next to me seemed to be having a good time as they snuggled on their bench. I watched as the man got down on his knee.

'Elizabeth, I have been a fool. I left you behind while I went on business trips and travelled the world. What I realized was the fact that there is no place I would rather be than with you. There is no other woman who can ever come close to who you are or what you represent for me. You are my everything and you always will be. Without you I have no purpose to live, breathe or go on. I love you. Will you marry me?'

Elizabeth, the lady who was sitting next to him, was too happy to say a word.

Love is a peculiar thing, I mused, watching them embrace. *When you love, you have so much to be grateful for and to live for, but when you lose it, you go on with every single day as if you are just a shell. Survival is the only reason one is on this earth. It has nothing to do with the fact that you feel anything as powerful as love any longer.*

'Oh, Steve! I love you too.' I heard her words, tight with emotion.

~

'It is a beautiful day. What are you doing here? Are you travelling for business as well?' An old man dressed in a business suit asked me as he sat on the bench beside me. I hadn't asked him to join me as I munched on a chocolate croissant that morning, but I didn't mind the intrusion at all. I realized, with a pang in my heart, that I was lonely.

I shook my head and tilted my bag of pastries towards him in invitation. He grinned and reached in and pulled out a pain au chocolat. He held it up in a silent toasting gesture and took a healthy bite. 'Mm,' he mumbled as crumbs fell onto his lap. 'Thank you my friend. I owe you a coffee for this treat. But please, tell me, why are you in beautiful Paris?'

'I quit my job to travel,' I explained, setting my own croissant on my lap. 'I have seen some incredible places, and

Paris seems to be one of the most amazing cities I have seen with my own eyes. There is nothing that could ruin this day and the beauty that it holds,' I said.

The man laughed. 'You have never been in love obviously. Every time I was away from my young bride, it would nearly kill me. There was something inside of me that I couldn't replace. It was as if I couldn't survive without her.'

'That is the problem. *I have loved, and that is why I am travelling. I am trying to escape,*' I admitted quietly.

The old man shook his head slowly. 'No matter what your thoughts are on women, let me tell you what I have learned about them. I have quite a bit of experience since my hair is turning white,' he joked.

'Please,' I invited. 'I am interested in your thoughts.'

He took another large bite of the pastry before he spoke. 'My Nancy was a lot like you. She was everything a man could ever dream of. I was nearly overwhelmed when I realized how much I fancied her. I was also a fool for not telling her how much I cared earlier. When I finally did, her past took on a life of itself and she allowed it to get between us. She loved someone who left her life in such an uproar that it scarred her beautiful heart.'

I winced, thinking of Nisha. I wondered how she and Kabir were doing. *Were they married yet?*

He continued. 'No matter what I told her, the scars were deep, and it took a long time for her to open her heart. By then we both had careers, and we got married. Now, as time has passed, I would do anything if I could just have her back.'

'What happened?' I asked.

'She divorced me,' the old man sighed. 'She could never forget the man who broke her heart, and she refused to let my love heal her.'

I looked down at the freshly-cut grass under my feet. Before I could say anything, the old man continued.

'Remember, my friend. Love is the strangest thing. When you have love, you will be over the moon and it will seem as if nothing can stop you. Love is something that opens your eyes to new discoveries, even in old places. You want to discover the wonders of the world all over again with the person who holds your heart in their own. When you lose it, all that once seemed to make the world around you will shatter.

'When you love someone, time is no object, but the memories are always stamped in your heart. I think it would be foolish for you to be so young and try to escape already what love has to offer. Don't make the same mistakes I made in my past! Go out there and live and love. In the end, we always regret the choices we didn't make, the love we didn't accept and the dreams we didn't fight for.

'When feelings are pure and the heart is true, even God is forced to change destiny,' he grinned.

My curiosity was certainly piqued. 'But can I give up

all this?' I asked, gesturing at the scene in front of us. 'All I've ever wanted was to travel. Should I give it all up for one woman? And what if she is the wrong woman for me?'

'Son,' he said, patting me on the knee, 'some women can steal your heart by their beauty, some can steal your mind by their intelligence and others can steal your soul by their presence. But if you meet the one who can steal your everything without doing anything, that's the one made for you.'

He stood and brushed the crumbs from his suit. 'Why would you chase your dreams alone when you can have your soul mate beside you?' He reached out and I shook his hand.

'You make some very good points,' I agreed. 'Thank you.'

He smiled. 'Maybe you can wait for days, weeks, months, years or even decades. You can waste so much time by just looking at the calendar and let all the tiny precious moments slip by. But for some of us, there's only now, only today. And the truth is, you never really know when God might need back the ones we love. So cherish every moment and everyone in your life.'

The old man left me wondering. Perhaps he was right.

I was not done travelling yet, though. There were more places I was desperate to explore. My plane landed in Halifax, Nova Scotia and I rented a car. I had heard people refer to parts of Cape Breton Island as the edge of the world. I wanted to see it before I returned to India. Later in the day,

I crossed the swing bridge over the Canso Causeway and arrived on the island, smiling as the fog drifted around me.

The following day, I teetered on the edge of the cliff of a campground at Meat Cove, watching the surf pummel the boulders below me. The sunshine was comforting on my back, its rays wrapping over my shoulders.

The air around me was void of human voices and any mechanical sounds. Here, at the northern tip of Cape Breton Island, I truly felt as if I was at the edge of the world. I looked to my left, taking in the gentle slope that curved out of sight. It looked safe, but I knew the perception was false, and that the land abruptly fell away into the cold waters below. To my right there was a small beach, dwarfed by threatening boulders above it. While the tiny area looked peaceful, the boulders peppering the sand indicated how treacherous the area was.

I threw my head back until the sun at my back heated my upturned face. *How long have I been running?* I asked myself, finally giving life to the spark of loneliness that had been threatening to ignite. My mind pondered over the last moments with Meera. If I closed my eyes, I could feel her lips gently brushing the tender spot behind my earlobe. Absently, my hand reached up to touch that very spot, but my touch brought no satisfaction. I needed her; I needed that beautiful, brown-eyed creature that I had thrown away.

At moments like this, I wondered if I'd made a mistake

in leaving Meera. My chin dropped to my chest in defeat. All this travelling, all the breathtaking sights I'd seen had been worthless alone. 'Seeing the world,' I muttered, my voice foreign in my ears. 'For nothing! I've been such a coward, running ... for what? And from what?'

Absently, I threaded my fingers through the grass beside me, imagining the blades were Meera's fingers. How selfish I'd been. I wanted her, but I didn't deserve to ever hear her soft laugh again. Not after I'd left her, walking out of her life without even saying goodbye.

I no longer saw the beauty in front of me. Instead, I conjured an image of my beloved Meera. *She was sitting in her dark room, tears flowing hotly down her cheeks. Her hair was dishevelled and her proud shoulders were pressed down by the enormity of her sorrow.* I had done that to her.

I heard a tearing sound as the vista returned to my sight. I looked down and realized I was holding a handful of grass, pulled by its roots in my own frustration.

I stood quickly, almost unaware of the treacherous drop in front of me. In a more rational mind, I would be terrified at how easily I could plunge to my death. But I was not rational now. I was desperate to return to my place. The moment I realized I could only be truly whole when I returned to Meera, the loneliness took form and pressed against me so I could barely breathe. I needed to find her.

MEERA

17

SOMETIMES

As the moon gradually wanes, so did my pain. The hole that Vivaan left when he disappeared was still there, although it was often filled, as a hole in the ground may be filled with rainwater.

Sometimes the hole in my heart was filled with a blinding red anger and I was furious with Vivaan for his abrupt departure.

Sometimes the hole was filled with a hot determination to move forward and live my life, convinced that I would never, ever utter his name again, not to Kabir and Nisha, and not in my most private moments. During these times, I would deliberately put his unfinished book in my garbage, certain that was where it should be. It might be minutes, or hours, but I always took the book back out.

Sometimes sadness just erupted and I would curl up, holding my knees to my chest, and rock gently on my bed.

Some days, I understood. After all, to love is to understand and set your love free to chase his dreams.

Sometimes, I simply did not care. About him, about my friends, about work. I would call office with a dumb excuse and spend the day roaming some remote place outside Pune. If Vivaan was so interested in escaping, I could escape as well.

I started doing some stupid things, like walking down the streets alone at night. I was always warned not to go out by myself at night, but I didn't care anymore.

Sometimes, I would creep in the shadows if I saw someone approaching on the sidewalk, but when I was alone, I treasured the solitude, the quiet, the dark.

When I returned to my apartment after walking for hours, I would chastise myself for taking such a risk by going out so late at night. Alone. The news was full of horrible stories; women mugged, assaulted ... or worse. I was lucky not to be approached, I would tell myself. Never again!

And then the next night, I would be tossing and turning in bed until I finally gave in to the temptation for another night-time stroll.

I simply did not care anymore.

VIVAAN

18

MISSING

I quit my job at Citibank and all I wanted was to travel. And yet I felt guilty, and there was nothing I could tell myself to justify the regret I felt that I hadn't said goodbye.

Every day I scoured this Earth to find happiness. I didn't find it or anything else to soothe my soul at all. I found wonderful places.

This was the opportunity I would have done anything for. I got to escape, but here I was, a stranger in a strange place. I was just a drifter who never stayed too long, and no one seemed to be curious about my story the way Meera had been.

I remembered asking her about her writing once.

'I'm sort of jealous,' I admitted. 'I am great at numbers and figures, but I don't think I'm any good at putting words together. You can write and your heart sings on the paper.'

'I want to inspire people with my writing. I want to touch

their souls,' she said. 'I want them to say, she feels us, she moves us.'

I could hear her voice, but when I tried to picture her smile, I struggled to call her up in my mind. I wished I had a picture of her, but no camera could ever capture the look in her eyes and the feelings in her heart when she looked at me.

Yes, I finally started to admit, I needed Meera in my life.

What had come over me? *I had promised myself never to fall in love!* But I broke my promise when I looked deep into Meera's eyes. She was the universe in which I was discovering myself for the first time. She was the most amazing woman, with a face of an angel. Her curiosity about the world around her always seemed to be empowering topics that would fascinate me for hours.

I remembered how thoughts of her came to me during my journeys. Shivering in Alaska, the northern lights reminded me of the green jade necklace she liked to wear.

In Cape Breton Island, I sat on the edge of a cliff, threading my fingers through the grass, and remembered when we walked to the park together, holding hands. The day she took her sandals off and walked barefoot. The day I kissed her. I closed my eyes. I could feel the softness of her lips on mine.

I thought of the little girl in Boston and how much Meera would have loved playing with the green balloon dog in the pool with her. She had a way of grabbing the important things in life and not worrying about what other people thought.

Every stop on my journey, Meera was with me. I might have been trying to escape from everything when I left India without saying goodbye, but somehow, Meera had followed me everywhere.

Meera. She always came into the café with such a bubbly personality. There was nothing that could or would stop her. There was nothing that could keep her down. She always wore a smile on her face; it made you feel like life would always be a wonderful place to live in.

Suddenly, I realized I didn't care about travelling. I missed her and I missed my life in India. The fact was, for so long I'd cared only about travelling, I didn't realize there was more to discuss and more to say to one another.

I never really left the café, but watched from afar as she looked around for me. When I asked her how her day was, she would always answer with, 'My day is better now that you are here.'

~

Every sunset I saw from different places of the world only reminded me of all the times I'd spent with Meera. We were in different cities, across the world from each other, and you can call it silly, but it felt as if we were still connected by each sunrise and each sunset.

I had left without a trace, without a goodbye and without telling anyone. *But I had my reasons.* I wished I could tell them to Meera. I thought about what the man in the park in Paris had said to me: 'In the end, we always regret the choices we didn't make, the love we didn't accept and the dreams we didn't fight for.'

I needed to get back to my friends. All of them: Kabir, Nisha and Meera. I hoped my abrupt departure hadn't damaged our friendships. And if it had, I needed to go back as soon as possible to ask for forgiveness.

MEERA

19

Healing

One morning I woke up to find the ache in my chest was not as sharp as the day before. I stretched and realized that I had finally slept through the entire night without interruption. No tossing and turning, no crying.

I got out of bed and dressed, actually looking forward to the day in front of me.

I can't believe it, I thought. *Am I starting to put Vivaan behind me? Have I begun to accept that he is not coming back?*

I took a quick shower, truly looking at myself in the mirror for the first time in a long time. My hair was longer than I liked and I could really use a good facial.

I wrinkled my nose at myself in the mirror. 'Time to really clean yourself up,' I said. Enough was enough, I decided. I did a quick Internet search and picked up the phone to make a call.

An hour later, I was walking into one of Pune's spas.

The gold and brown tones of the reception area calmed me immediately. I was greeted by a soft-spoken woman who confirmed my appointment on her computer.

I was taken into a room and offered a soft, white robe as the different spa packages were explained to me at length. I opted for a relaxing aromatherapy massage and felt some of the stress that had built up in me slowly start to be rubbed out of my muscles.

I dozed to the soft music and the sound of water.

That afternoon, I continued my day of pampering, driving to my favourite salon for a facial, manicure and haircut.

I topped my day off with a shopping trip where I found a beautiful teal sundress.

That evening, I went to Kafe Kabir to show off my successful day. I grinned as Kabir saw me walk in and let out a long whistle. I watched Nisha shoot him a scowl before she followed the direction in which his eyes were looking.

'Meera!' she cooed. 'You look beautiful!'

I couldn't help myself. I spun around like I'd stepped out of a magazine page.

Nisha rushed over and hugged me. 'What happened to you? What a transformation! Has something happened?'

She wrapped her arm around mine and escorted me over to the counter, babbling happily. Kabir kept smiling and leaned across the counter for a quick hug.

'Doesn't she look amazing?' Nisha said.

Kabir nodded. 'You do, Meera. I am so happy to see this change in you. Did anything happen?' he asked curiously.

'If you mean, did I hear from anyone special, the answer is no,' I said pointedly. 'I just woke up today and felt like it was time to stop moping around. I realized I was looking pretty scruffy, so I went to get my hair done.'

'Not just your hair,' Nisha commented.

'No,' I admitted. 'I got a massage and a facial … and then I went shopping.' I grinned.

'I thought that was a new dress,' Kabir said.

Nisha gave him a shove. 'Since when do men notice things like that?' she asked playfully.

'Since I met you,' he said and blew her a kiss.

I was caught up in the aura of happiness; I couldn't help laughing, and then laughing some more for the sheer joy of the sound.

'I'm still so surprised,' Nisha said. 'You are so transformed. And I don't mean on the outside. You are different on the inside, too. You are almost glowing.'

'I don't know,' I said. 'I just woke up feeling like the old Meera again. I had a long talk with myself and said, "You need to be real and true to yourself. Don't run away from yourself, your dreams or the life which you deserve. Yes, you can still live more, learn more and love more than you've done so far. You have nothing to lose and everything to gain. Wake up and run towards the beautiful life you deserve."'

'Wow,' Nisha murmured. 'You are amazing.'

'I think we need to celebrate,' Kabir decided and Nisha clapped her hands. 'It's pretty quiet in here right now … the crew we have can handle it for a few hours. Let's go grab dinner.'

Nisha squeezed my arm. 'I'm happy for you, Meera.'

'I am too,' Kabir seconded. 'Our treat. Let's go eat!'

We had a wonderful meal and laughed a lot. It felt so good to be joking around again. When we finished, I thanked my friends for a wonderful meal.

'Come back to the café,' Nisha invited. 'I'll buy you a cappuccino. I know the owner,' she teased, winking.

'Thank you, but I think I'm going to head back to my apartment. I left my writing things there and I feel like I want to go back and write.'

They both hugged me. 'This has been a great evening,' Kabir said.

As I headed home, I wondered what Vivaan was doing. I realized I could think about him without that deep, biting hurt that I'd been carrying for months.

VIVAAN

20

THE PUBLISHER

When the plane finally touched down in India, I took a taxi directly to Kafe Kabir.

Nothing had changed in the café. It was the same lively place that was packed full house. The coffee smell was tantalizing. I wanted my beloved black coffee, but there was something I wanted even more.

'Hi Nisha, is Meera here?' I asked, as Nisha looked at me as if she'd seen a ghost. She stood there in utter shock. I hugged her and asked again, 'Is she here?'

'No, you just missed her. She went with Kabir to the publisher. We are all hoping that they like her book.' Her voice took on a chastising tone. 'You would have known this if you had tried to contact her instead of just vanishing.'

I groaned. I knew she was right, but did she have to point out what I had done?

'She cried every single day after you left, Vivaan. You

broke her into so many little pieces. Vivaan ... really ... how could you do that to her? To us?'

Nisha passed me a cup of black coffee. I sipped it gratefully, although the thought crossed my mind that she might have spit in it. 'I honestly think she would have handled it a bit better if you'd at least said goodbye to her. It was the fact you didn't tell her that you were leaving. You told no one you were leaving, Vivaan. No one knew you quit your job at Citibank until Meera and Kabir went to see you.'

'They went to see me?' I asked, confused.

'Yes, of course they went to see you and that was how they found out. Meera cared about you. We all cared about you, Vivaan. You didn't even tell us you were closing all your emails, and you turned off your phone. She waited for a message from you every day. Every single day. She never received one. She hung on to those broken dreams which seemed to be spinning her around.'

'I don't understand. I thought Meera and I were just friends,' I whispered.

'Friends say goodbye to one another. Friends talk. Friends explain things. If your idea of friendship is just walking out one day, you need to go back to school and learn what it really means to have friends.

'Vivaan, you just left without a word. What you did was escape because you didn't want to deal with something. That is what you are very good at, isn't that what you said in the beginning? You didn't even say goodbye to Kabir or me. I thought you two shared something special. You might have only been financially contributing, but to Kabir, you were true partners. I guess you proved with your mysterious persona that you have more to you than just who you had everyone believing you were.'

I hung my head. I knew I had a lot to do to make up for all the hurt I had caused, but to hear Nisha lay it out in front of me like that made me feel so ashamed.

She walked around the counter and wrapped her arms around me. For a second, I froze. Here this woman was, yelling at me for leaving, and then she was hugging me?

'Most of all, Vivaan,' she continued. '*Friends forgive.*'

We hugged for several moments as I felt her anger subside. I cared about Nisha, so her forgiveness was the most beautiful gift she could offer.

Suddenly, I realized who Nisha was referring to. I knew who the publisher was. 'Nisha,' I began in a rush, 'you are right. I made a huge mistake, and I want to make it right. I'm sorry to run off again, but I need to find Kabir and Meera.'

'Good luck,' I heard her call after me.

This publisher was a friend of Kabir's that he had often gone on and on about to Meera. He always promised that he would one day schedule a meeting between them.

I walked into the receptionist's small office. No one was there at the desk, so I walked on towards the office where the publisher and editor sat. They made the decision on whether to publish a book or not. I could hear voices through the partially-closed door.

'I have to admit, Meera, even though this is your first book, I do like it. It's fascinating and well-written. You have no experience in this field, yet it seems that something very special has inspired you, and it touched your heart in the deepest way. You got the readers to feel through the words that are on the pages. You can feel the love that is forming between your two main characters, Vivaan and Meera. You showed us that sometimes the smallest changes in life are where the largest impacts come from. You created this mysterious man who falls in love with a girl who loves to write. I am stunned by the plot line and love it beyond words,' the publisher said from the other side of the door.

I gloated in the hallway as I listened.

'There is one problem,' the publisher finally said after a long pause.

'What would that be?' Meera asked.

'The book isn't finished. You ended it where Vivaan leaves. You never showed what happens to Vivaan. All you have shown is the fact that they fall in love, and he gets up one day and never contacts her. That was the ending of the book. What happens to Vivaan? Does he embark on that world journey? Does he ever return? If he doesn't return, does Meera begin to love someone else?'

'I ... I don't know what happened to Vivaan,' Meera whispered.

'This would just be a waste of time if you don't finish it. We cannot publish a book that is unfinished. I understand that sometimes, in life, the smallest things make the largest impact, but you must finish the book properly if you want me to publish it.'

I quickly barged in. 'Vivaan is here. Turn around and look at me. I am back, and now I want you to finish the book.'

Meera stared at me, her beautiful black hair accenting a face that had gone shockingly pale. I stared, waiting for her to move. Finally, she shot out of her chair. 'Vivaan!' Meera shouted.

'Meera, I am back,' I said with a smile.

Meera burst into tears and started leaving. I reached out and pulled her to me before she could walk through the door. I would not let her escape as I had.

I held her hands and said. 'Maybe we should go to Kafe Kabir and have a cup of coffee so we can all know about my explorations.'

Kabir didn't say anything, he just hugged me, and then we all made our way to Kafe Kabir.

~

'I wanted to tell you that I am incredibly sorry for just vanishing like that,' I began when I was settled at a table with my beloved friends. 'I wasn't thinking about the fact that it would hurt you; those were never my intentions. The choices I made while leaving were very wrong. I never said goodbye to you or Kabir and Nisha.' I nodded to each as I spoke their names.

'That was a choice I have regretted every single day that I have been gone. I should have told you that my travels seemed to be calling, beckoning … and that it was my time to embark on my dream.' I sighed, running my thumb over Meera's beautiful, long fingers. 'It was a great adventure. I saw a beautiful sunset while in Paris and I missed you so badly. I wanted you there to share it with me.'

I searched her face, her eyes, for a hint of how she was feeling.

She was still silent.

'Tomorrow I want to see you. I have something important to tell you,' I ducked my head and whispered in her ear. Then, louder, I said with a smile, 'But tonight you can pick my brain about all my adventures,' and began narrating the memoirs of my travels.

One more day and Meera would know the truth. It was something that had been weighing on my mind lately, and I was nervous about it. But, after the encounter I'd had with the older gentleman in Paris, I knew it was time to tell Meera everything about me and my feelings.

21

THE WEDDING

By the time I got back to the corner table in the café the next day, I had realized that Meera wasn't happy to see me. She was upset and angry, but didn't speak of it.

'You have something to tell me?' she asked.

'Yes,' I began nervously. 'I thought I should explain to you why I left without telling you anything.' I sensed that she was expecting something else and I let out a sigh and held her hand.

In her other hand, I placed a marriage card dated for 2012, three years ago.

Her eyes were filled with confusion, then anger as she read the names out loud.

'Vivaan weds Radha? You were married?' she asked with such anger in her tone.

'Meera,' I begged, 'will you please let me tell you the story before you react? It isn't what you think.'

'What I think?' Her voice rose an octave. 'You don't even want to know what I think!'

I blocked out her anger as I continued. 'I had been in love before, and it was too painful to talk about when you wanted to know my story. So I showed you in Kabir's eyes, his love story. Don't get me wrong, love is a wonderful thing! It is the beating of two hearts as they play the same song. I went to college with Radha. Everything was going great. We exchanged numbers and our relationship started blossoming into something more. We fell madly in love with one another; it was the type that made you feel dizzy.' I took a deep breath. 'We decided to get married.'

I could see Meera breaking down, but I had to continue.

'I was so excited when she agreed to marry me. She was beautiful, funny and very intelligent. She always tried to help people in all possible ways.'

'Vivaan,' Meera said coldly. 'I truly do not want to hear how in love you were!'

'Please, just hear me out,' I said, grabbing her hand to keep her from standing up.

She pulled her hand away from mine, but nodded. 'Fine. I'll listen,' she huffed.

'Thank you,' I responded. 'The wedding plans moved forward. Everything was coming together so beautifully.'

Meera groaned. Did she just roll her eyes? I wasn't sure. I knew I was upsetting her, but I really needed to push on and tell her the full story. She deserved to hear it.

I shuddered, bracing myself to tell her the rest of the story. I took a deep drink of water and pressed on.

'The day of the wedding came. I went to Pingale Garden where we were to be married. I was so excited; I couldn't wait to see my bride.' I took a deep breath. 'But she never came.'

Meera gasped in surprise.

'I tried calling her but she didn't pick up her phone. We waited for half an hour, then an hour. I was frantic. Radha was always on time and it was, after all, her wedding day.'

'What happened?' Meera asked quietly.

'She was missing for three days. I couldn't eat, I couldn't sleep. Nothing. The police came and for a few horrible moments, I was a suspect in her disappearance. Can you imagine? The woman I was to marry disappeared, and if that wasn't bad enough, I was accused of some crime!'

Meera shook her head violently. 'I cannot imagine,' she said. 'What a horrible thing for you to have had to deal with.'

I took a shuddering sigh. 'They finally found her body...'

'Her body? Vivaan, oh no.'

I nodded. 'She was on her way to the wedding and she wanted a few moments to herself. She was already dressed in her beautiful gown, with a stunning diamond necklace and earrings.'

My voice became flat, even to my ears. 'She was raped and murdered.'

'No!' Meera screamed.

'Yes,' I said with tears in my eyes. 'Her body was found in a park, half undressed. The jewellery was taken; even the earrings were ripped out of her ears!' I said angrily.

'Please, please tell me you were never accused of it.'

'No. I was at the wedding venue when she was ... killed.'

'Did they find who did it?'

'Eventually, they did.'

Meera didn't say a word. She didn't say she was sorry about what I'd gone through, like she had about Nisha's abortion or Kabir's story. She just sat there.

'So that's it,' I said and sighed again. 'Now you know why I can never return your affection, Meera. I am so sorry.'

'Are you okay?' Meera asked softly.

'I will be one day,' I responded. 'For now I just keep these memories tucked away in my heart. I never want to forget Radha and the love we had.'

I realized at that moment that my hands were shaking, and I was covered with sweat.

'The fateful day still haunts me. I wish that you could have met her,' I said. 'I know that's weird, but she touched so many people.'

Meera squeezed my hand, the only thing she did as her eyes had tears in them. She swallowed hard to prevent herself from crying.

'I was lost without her, Meera,' I said. 'And I still am.'

Meera was now crying as hard as I was. We both seemed

to be feeling the pain of love. I didn't mean to make her cry again; I really didn't. But she needed to know my story and whom my heart had belonged to and always would belong to.

'I understand that you loved Radha and that you will always have a special place in your heart for her,' Meera finally said.

'I told you it wasn't what you thought. I never cheated on Radha in your company. I have no girlfriend or woman on Earth who inhabits that spot. This is why I decided to travel. I couldn't handle all the memories and nightmares that surround me with Radha. She surrounds me in every breath of Pune and India. She was what kept this place lively for me. There is nothing that has kept me here since. I travelled to try and free myself from the pain that I am constantly in from her loss.'

Meera nodded slowly as if she understood. I wasn't sure if she did or if she was just agreeing.

She wrapped her tiny hand around mine. 'I am sorry beyond words that you lost your bride on the day of your wedding. Radha sounds like she was a wonderful woman. She was very lucky to have you as her fiancé for the time you two had together. I know she would be happy with whomever you find after.'

'That's what I need to explain to you, I need to make you understand that I cannot love anyone else. I am too heartbroken and still in love with Radha. You must know why I cannot commit to you. I can't give you the love which you deserve. I am already committed to Radha, and you deserve someone who should be committed to you fully. I have enjoyed your company and the time we spent together; do not ever get me wrong on that. I just can't love you the way I love Radha.'

Meera stood up then, and asked, 'Why did you give me all those gifts? Why did you care so much? Why did you kiss me? Didn't you love me ever? Not for a single moment?'

Before I could answer, she left.

MEERA

22

THE CLIMB

His revelations were too much for me to bear. Yes, I understood Vivaan's love, and as he'd explained what happened to Radha, his running made so much sense.

Because I loved him, I wanted to stay and comfort him, but also because I loved him, I needed to escape myself and process the story that he had told me.

Tears streaming down my face, I ran to my car and began to drive. Where, I didn't know, but as long as there was a road in front of me, I would keep going.

Sometimes I took a road on the right, sometimes on the left. Most of the time, I just kept driving on a straight path.

Suddenly, I realized I was in Gunjawane. Somewhere above me was Rajgad, an ancient fort. I hadn't been there in years, but the old stone paths were calling to me.

Before I left my car, I tapped out a quick message to Nisha. *'I'm okay,'* I typed. *'Going to climb to Rajgad. Will let you know when I'm down. Don't worry.'*

The climb was not too difficult, but I was glad I had sensible shoes on. I went up the path quickly, and enjoyed the burn in my legs as I climbed. I needed to feel that pain. I needed to feel alive.

As I approached the fort, my lungs were burning, and I slowed down as I navigated the well-worn path through a meadow.

Reaching Rajgad, a soft rain began to fall, cooling my overheated body. I stopped at one of the water tanks and took a long drink of water before I went forward.

As I rested, I thought about Vivaan and Radha. I loved him, but could I settle for being his friend? Did I dare reveal the depth of my feelings to him? And if he did return some of my affection, would I be chasing the ghost of Radha all the time?

My tears started to flow again as the rain fell harder. I wanted to talk to Vivaan again and thought about turning back to descend the path. No. I had come this far and the path to Chor Darwaja was close. I had never taken this path before because it was a steep climb. But the idea of seeing the 'hidden door' tempted me on. Perhaps, if I made it to that door, I could find the hidden door to Vivaan's heart? It was foolish, but I was beyond rational at that point.

I began to climb the steep, rocky path, clutching tightly to the metal railing.

What was that? I thought I heard my name being called out. But that was impossible.

On a particularly difficult part, I stopped, breathless. I needed to rest; my legs were wobbly and the rain had made the rocks slippery. As I recovered a little, I turned around to take in the beautiful view. Ah ... I felt like I could touch heaven from here.

I smiled, a contented peace taking over my body, but then I thought of Vivaan and realized how wrong I was to run away. I closed my eyes and saw the pain in his. Yes, he loved her. He was capable of great love, but that immense love also made him vulnerable to immense pain.

It must have taken so much courage to open up and tell me about Radha. He ran halfway around the world to avoid his memories of her, but he came back and chose to face those memories to tell me about them.

And when he finally managed to tell me, how did I respond? I took all that pain and turned my back. I could barely acknowledge the horror that he had gone through, and the effort it took for him to recall that day; I'd crumbled up the story and thrown it back at him.

I felt such shame. All I could think about were his words when he'd said he could not love me. That intimate conversation, his loved one, raped and murdered on his wedding day ... all of it was eclipsed by my reaction when he said he couldn't love me.

I needed to get back to him. To apologize, to heal him. I wanted to remind him that life should go on. We lost, we mourned, but as long as we lived, we could love again.

I nodded firmly. It was time to go back to Kafe Kabir.

It happened so suddenly. I let go of the metal railing to brush the damp hair from my face as I took one last look at the view. I began to focus on the steep steps I needed to descend, when my foot slipped on the rock. I started to fall, reaching desperately for the railing, but my hand couldn't find it in my blind search.

I began to tumble, the rocks smashing my body and I let out a terrified scream.

Mercifully, darkness came rushing and I felt no more pain.

VIVAAN

23

OBLIVION

Meera left in such a hurry that I knew I'd hurt her. I started to rush after her, but I didn't think I could do her much good while I was in such a state myself. I had pulled off a long-guarded bandage and showed her the deep wound that I had hidden from her for so long.

I went for a long walk, trying to collect my thoughts. I wanted to be in a better frame of mind when she came back.

Hours later I returned and went back to the table in the corner. Kabir grabbed the seat that had been occupied by Meera.

'I heard your whole story and what you told Meera,' Kabir said and then took a deep breath. 'Please don't take this the wrong way, but I want you to know how proud I am of you that you faced your past and told Meera about your Radha.'

I winced, hearing Kabir say her name. But I nodded. 'Thank you, my friend. And now you know why I ran, too. I owe you an apology as well for not saying goodbye. I treated your friendship badly.'

'We all make mistakes, Vivaan,' he responded. 'And we move past them. You are a dear friend and I am happy you're back.'

I took a sip, glad to have our friendship on good terms once more.

Kabir continued. 'Meera loves you very much.'

I sighed. 'I already told her that I cannot feel the same way for her.'

Kabir shook his head. 'That's the point I am trying to make. You love her just as much as she loves you. I don't understand why you are locking up your heart, Vivaan. You are punishing yourself! You don't need to love her like Radha; you just need to love her like Meera,' Kabir pointed out.

'That's the thing I was trying to tell her,' I said, frustrated. 'I can't love anyone. Period. That is why I left without saying goodbye. I know she likes me, but I can't love her back.'

A shadow on the backdoor caught my eye. I thought for sure I'd seen someone standing there, but I guess it was just the way the light had hit it.

'I loved Radha and will always love her. I cannot just turn

a switch and say that I will not love her anymore. I know Meera was pretty upset and angry with me, but I decided it was best to be upfront about this.'

Kabir looked at me with his eyebrows raised in disapproval. 'Do you know the worst thing a man can do to a woman?'

I shrugged. 'I am assuming it is being unfaithful.'

'No, it is making her fall in love with you when you have no intentions of loving her back.'

I looked down without making eye contact with Kabir. He was right. I felt shame erupt in me once again.

~

'Kabir! Vivaan! We must get to the hospital quickly!' Nisha said as she hung up the phone. My heart lurched as I heard the terror in her voice.

'Why? What is going on?' I asked.

'It is Meera! She was in an accident.'

Without another word, we all rushed out of the café and got into Kabir's car.

'Where was she?' I demanded.

'She went to Rajgad,' Nisha said.

'Rajgad?' I yelled. 'Why did she go there? And what happened?'

Nisha shook her head. 'I don't know, Vivaan. Let's get to the hospital and find out what happened.'

How could this have happened? Was she very angry and not paying attention? I thought.

We reached the hospital and inquired about Meera. Minutes slipped into hours as we waited desperately outside the emergency ward for the doctor to come out and tell us something. I just knew there was an accident. I felt as if I was helpless again, as I was when Radha disappeared. There was nothing I could do for Meera as she lay in that room.

Tragedy surrounded those I loved and I couldn't help but wonder why.

I continued to pace. Then I sat back down, wrapping my arms around me. I cried, rocking myself back and forth in the chair.

'Tell me again, Nisha,' I said when I could speak again. 'Rajgad?'

'That's what her text said,' Nisha responded, her voice thick with tears. Kabir held her tighter.

'But why?'

'She was escaping,' Kabir said. It was too ironic. I dropped my head to my chest and started sobbing.

I felt a hand on my shoulder and looked up. Nisha was trying to get my attention because the doctor was approaching us. I was hopeful and terrified at the same time as I searched his face for some sign.

'She has been stabilized,' the doctor said quietly. 'Her

body is badly broken, but we have done all we can for now.'

'What happened?' I demanded.

'I'm not sure. The reports are that she somehow fell while climbing to the fort. Luckily some other hikers were close by and called the emergency personnel. A helicopter got to her pretty quickly and brought her here. Please excuse me; I need to get back.'

'Can I go in and talk to her?' I asked.

'Sir,' he said cautiously, 'she is stabilized, but at the moment, she is still unconscious. She will not be talking to you until she gains consciousness. We're moving her to the Intensive Care Unit.'

'Intensive Care Unit?' Kabir said. 'I thought you said she was stable?'

'She is stable enough that we can move her. She is still in a serious condition. But she is unconscious, and the longer she is unconscious, the greater the chance that there are critical problems that are life-threatening.'

The doctor's words ripped out my heart.

How long had I been there? Was it hours? Minutes? I couldn't remember as I looked around and followed the doctors after they moved Meera to the Intensive Care Unit. People seemed to be suffering in this ward. Every single one of them was facing a life-and-death condition. Some were ill from diseases, while others were like Meera, broken from accidents.

Meera's face was swollen, and her eyelids were shut. Her head was wrapped in bandages, and she was hooked to machines that made her breathe. I didn't know what all the machines did, but I knew that the sounds were driving me nuts. I felt as if this was my fault. I wasn't the person she thought she had known. I was the person who told her about Radha and broke her heart. She stormed off in her car, climbed the fort and ended up in an accident; now I was praying for her life.

'I will stay here. Please, go home and rest. I want to be with her when she wakes up,' I said firmly to Kabir and Nisha.

I sat in a chair next to Meera. IVs were in her delicate hand and a breathing tube was in her mouth.

I felt that she was in a state of oblivion, a web of medical instruments trying to keep her alive. My eyes stared at the blinking red and green lights as she fought for her existence. I realized I was fighting for my breath as well.

'What I have done?' I said softly to her. I had a chance to feel love again, and this is how I treated it. Kabir was right; the worst thing a man could do was make a woman fall in love with him and have no intention to love her back. That was what I had done to Meera.

I held her hand as I started sobbing next to her. My eyes were locked on her and I was silently begging her to respond. Her eyes didn't flicker. The noises of the machines told me what her body wasn't doing for her. It tore me apart seeing her in this condition.

'Meera!' I said. 'I gifted you things because I loved you. I cared for you because I loved you. I kissed you because I loved you. I loved you every moment. I always had. That was the real reason I came back to India. I couldn't go a day without thinking about you. You were my whole world, and I felt so guilty that I was supposed to still love Radha. Oh, Meera! If I lose you, I lose my whole life. You gave me a reason to live. You got me to get up and chase my dreams. And now look at you. You are stuck in a hospital bed with tubes and machines keeping you alive. Wake up, my love. If you wake up, I can tell you everything and how I feel. I will find a way to deal with Radha's death. I just don't think I am going to be able to bear it if you die. I won't be able to handle it at all.'

Every so often nurses came in and worked on Meera. They would write on her clipboard. Some of the nurses tried to talk to me, others would ignore me. I didn't care. I held Meera's hand and refused to go anywhere. When the day become night, I propped myself up on the chair as I held her hand and would doze off. The sounds of the machines didn't give me a good night's sleep, but I wanted to be there, holding her hand, if she woke up. She would know the truth and know that deep down inside she could never replace Radha, but she could find another piece of my heart that would be just for her.

Some pieces of life find themselves so attached to our

mind that when they are gone, they remind us of themselves a lot more than before. Yet someday we will realize that every piece becomes blurry, every memory starts fading. Just like an old book.

24

SQUEEZE MY HAND

Hours turned into days and days turned into a week. I was exhausted and looked like hell when Kabir and Nisha came in and dropped off food for me.

'How is she?' Kabir asked.

I shrugged. 'The doctor said she has brain activity, which is good. Other than that, she still hasn't regained consciousness. She is still in a coma. I am scared of losing her. I should have told her how I really feel, but I was trying to protect myself from this. Here I am in a hospital room, going through this again.'

'Vivaan, you need to go home and shower. Take a few hours and go take care of yourself. You need to at least shave—you have a beard now,' Nisha pointed out.

'I can't go anywhere until Meera wakes up.' I felt almost childish as I made this announcement, but I couldn't bring myself to leave her side.

The nurses encouraged me to talk to her. Sometimes, I told her stories about my trip; other times, I just told her what was in my heart.

I admitted to her that, through my journeys, I realized that one can never run from one's own self, one's own soul.

'The day we met, I was almost frozen....You were so beautiful that I wanted to speak to you, but I was afraid to utter a word. I held my breath and wanted to stop time. Right from the start I knew that I had found a home for my heart.'

A nurse came in and I stopped talking. She gestured for me to continue.

'Meera, you turned my world upside down. You give me immense happiness … you are my soul. My love, I don't want to look back in five years' time and think, "We could have been magnificent, but I was afraid." In five years, I want to remember how fear tried to cheat me out of the best thing in my life. But I didn't let it.'

The nurse wrote something in Meera's chart. I didn't look at her directly, but I could see out of the corner of my eye that she was wiping away tears.

'Sweetheart,' I begged. 'Squeeze my hand. With it comes my heart, soul, love, trust, faith, hopes, dreams, past and future.

'Take my hand, and with it, all I have and all I am is forever yours.'

I didn't go anywhere; I didn't escape. Everyone thought I

should leave the room to do things. They told me the hospital would call me up if there were any changes. I didn't want a call from the hospital. I wanted to see her dark brown eyes look deep within my own.

MEERA

25

TRAPPED

I looked around, but nothing seemed familiar. Where was I? I tried to see the ground, but it did not seem to be under me.

I felt like I was nowhere, yet everywhere at the same time.

Am I floating?

My mind was a jumbled confusion.

Then I felt someone close. I knew who he was, although I couldn't see him.

'I see you, Vivaan,' I cried out.

'I feel you through this invisible distance between us. I see you through the words you utter beside me. Every time you keep a check on me, I feel your touch. But there is something missing. Something I cannot feel. It's your warmth.

'Some nights, when you hold my hands, I feel your tears running over my palm, over my hand. But I can't feel if it's warm or cold. Have I lost my ability to feel? Vivaan, tell me, why do I want to cry every time I see you sobbing. I try hard to weep and vent out all the frustration and anger burning inside me. But I fail, always.

'Vivaan, I am sorry, but I am scared. My only wish is to be able to move my hand and hold yours tight. I have tried my best to lift my fingers and tell you not to lose hope. But it is all in vain. I dream of how we met and the moments we spent together. I try to escape my reality right now and fall asleep to dream about us being together again. And yet when I wake up, what I see is this dark reality. I want to close my eyes and see the light within me but I cannot feel my eyes.

'Vivaan, I feel trapped within myself. Please help me.'

VIVAAN

26

A Forgotten Diary

The machines whirled on as Meera lay lifeless in the Intensive Care Unit. I wasn't sure how long I had been there. Nurses came in, checked Meera's stats and walked back out.

One day, a nurse—placing her hand on my shoulder—said, 'Her memories are intact. She remembers everything.'

I didn't know what to say, so I just nodded. It had been eight months since I had seen any signs of improvement in Meera's condition. I waited for the slightest hint of movement. But she just lay still.

I didn't leave Meera's side except to go to the bathroom. On occasion, a nurse would order me into a shower, and I would rush under the water. Sometimes I put my dirty clothes back on; other times, I was able to change into fresh clothes that Kabir brought.

I didn't go home. Nisha or Kabir would come in every day and bring me food around mealtimes. One day, they brought some of Meera's belongings, hoping to see her wake up. One of the things Nisha brought was her diary.

'Have there been any improvements?' Kabir asked one day.

I shook my head. 'No, but the doctor still says there is brain activity. He thinks that she listens to me when I read to her. I hope that is the truth. I am going to read her story out loud, and I hope before I finish it, she wakes up.'

Kabir bent down and gave me a hug before he left.

I began to ramble. 'Oh, Meera! I wish I had told you everything instead of acting the way I did. I was wrong! There's so much I want to tell you!'

I stroked her hair. 'I want to tell you all about why I returned to India, not to tell you about Radha, but because I love you. I love you more than I wanted to admit. There will always be a place in my heart for Radha, but there will be a different place here in my heart for you. Wake up so I can tell you in person.'

I wanted to see her dark brown eyes again just looking at me, but not even a flicker of life seemed to move inside her.

I let out a sigh. Kabir had been right—I was given such a gift. I wasn't cursed, but given another opportunity to love. I looked over at her. Her face was swollen, and her eyes were still shut as tubes helped her breathe. She wasn't the same angel-faced Meera that she was just before the accident when she was hurt and angry at me and stormed out of the café.

'My love,' I begged. 'Don't just breathe, live your life.'

Still, nothing.

I picked up her forgotten diary and looked at her. There had to be a way to help her through this. Even though she was in a coma, I would help her. I had no clue if it would make her come back to our world or not, but I started reading the story she had written out loud to her. Every single day she seemed to be unchanged by the world around her. I told her about the traveller in the café and how someday he would embark on this world adventure, but for now he took her hand in his and watched a sunset in Pune.

Then, I turned a page and found the entry for the day that Kabir had read out loud. Stuffed between the pages was the napkin that read 'BEAUTIFUL'. She was beautiful, and her writing was beyond beautiful … if only I could tell her again to her face when she was awake.

The journey with Vivaan, the traveller, seemed to keep going on. She had me doing and encountering all sorts of things. She had captured every moment as if her mind was a camera, and I was witnessing this for the very first time. I flipped through the book and found the entry from the day I'd left. The pages seemed tear-stained, and several pages had been removed. That was what she had thought was the end.

I knew I was no writer and I was far from being an author. I turned the page. 'Vivaan came back!' it read. It went into a descriptive passage on how I had surprised her.

I continued reading further, about how I wanted to meet her at the café and that I had something to tell her. *'I think he is finally going to admit he loves me! I think he might propose. I am so scared and excited that I have butterflies in my stomach.'*

I stopped reading. Unfortunately, that wasn't what happened. My eyes began to tear up all over again. What had I been thinking? How could I have been so ruthless?

27

You

Meera was still unconscious. My patience was finally wearing thin and I knew I was on the verge of breaking down. I had to express myself or I would go mad.

I held her hands, closed my eyes, and uttered the deepest feelings of my heart.

'*I was never a writer and I don't aspire to be one either. I was never a good reader and I don't know if I will ever be one. But now, I have been much more.*

'*Every day, I woke up; I tried to find reasons to live. Every night, when I slept, I tried to find reasons to not die. Every moment, I tried to find reasons to hope, dream and love. But I never found them. Until I met you.*

'*I saw chaos, confusion, and fear all around me. But not within me, after I met you.*

'*Time decides our fate, our journey. And when time changes, everything changes. Everything. Sometimes for worse,* sometimes for better. And sometimes, for the best. I never believed that. Until you happened to me.

'It's not a story and maybe it's not love. It's about something more real than stories and more powerful than love. It's about you. Yes, you. Real and powerful.

'I have never been happy with someone. I wanted to be with different people at different places with different feelings. I wanted to explore everything, know everyone. But then I explored you. And I found you are not just ONE, you are an infinity. An infinity of love, care, trust, respect, understanding. A universe of inspirations, aspirations, hope and happiness. Maybe you are the universe out there which I explore. Or the universe in me that I seek.

'You do not start, nor do you ever end. You are constant, yet ever changing. You are everywhere and yet just with me. You are my creator or my creation, I question myself.'

'Beautiful,' was the word I heard. Each syllable was laboured, forced and tired. I looked up, startled. There was my Meera, with tears in her eyes.

I didn't know what to say. Was it a miracle or the power of love? Was it all destined?

I kissed her, and kept my face close to hers as our tears mixed together.

Epilogue

Everyone Has a Story

Fate had drawn my story out of me. I knew when I met Vivaan that his story was the one I wanted to tell, but I could never have imagined the depths and layers that I would encounter.

I still had to walk with the support of a cane; my body was slower to recover from the fall than I wanted. I had broken multiple bones, my leg bearing the worst of the physical damage. I endured painful therapies and, at one point, I was told I may never walk again.

But I was determined that when I stood up in front of people at the café and read excerpts from my book, I would be standing in the truest sense, and not speaking from a wheelchair.

Almost two whole years had passed since the day I met Vivaan and his story began to spin in my mind. How young I'd felt then, intensely listening to Arjun Mehra and desperately wanting to become an author like him.

Now, I looked at all the people and my hands seemed to shake as I realized I would be in front of this crowd, entertaining them with my story and explaining how, two years ago, my life changed altogether. Vivaan noticed and extended a steadying hand out, squeezing mine encouragingly. The trembling stopped as I felt his energy and it gave me the strength I needed.

My book had finally been finished. It was no longer an incomplete book. I was surprised that the publisher had liked the idea that Vivaan contribute his perspective as well, and I was thrilled at the fact that, although I began this story, we finished it together.

'Stop worrying! You will be fine!' Vivaan whispered as he kissed me.

'You act like you are positive of that,' I whispered as I returned his kiss. 'I wish I had your courage.'

'I'll share,' he grinned. 'This time you won't be trying to face the crowd alone. We are going to be doing this together. But you, Miss Writer, will have to begin it yourself. You need to have your time on the stage by yourself. After all, this book would never have been written if it weren't for you.'

I smiled as I looked into his eyes. I loved the universe within them, the one that made me not only discover myself and my story, but also made me realize that shared happiness was the best type of dream come true.

Kabir pointed to his watch and motioned to me. He grinned and cleared his throat.

'Ladies and gentlemen,' he began loudly. 'It is finally the time that you have been waiting so long for. I am so excited to be standing here to introduce you to Meera, our own author. Meera began much like you, sitting in those very chairs over many long nights and weekends, writing a marvellous story,' Kabir said.

The crowd roared, clapping in excitement as I went up in front of everyone. My heart was beating fast, and I was sure somehow I was going to mess it up. My eyes searched the crowd. So many eyes were set on me, but then mine locked on Vivaan's. He nodded his encouragement.

'My name is Meera and I am the author of this book, *Everyone Has a Story*. Two years ago, I was sitting in a café, listening to an author, Arjun Mehra, talk about his writing. I was wrapped up in my own little world, listening so intently to the author. I was mesmerized, but unaware of the man behind me who wanted to travel the world. What I didn't realize at the time was that the curiosity of this man would take us through an amazing story of friendship, love and life. Neither one of us could have predicted how it would end,' I said.

I sipped some water and continued, 'Every single day, another page is added and as one chapter finishes, another one starts.

'Remember, everyone has a story. It might or might not be a love story. It could be a story of dreams, friendship, hope, survival or even death. And every story is worth telling. But more than that, it's worth living.

'If I have any words of advice for you, it is this: embrace every day, even the rough ones. Each day is your very own page, and you have the power to write the words on those pages. Be courageous, and be strong, but don't forget it is okay to be weak at times, too.'

I looked over at Kabir and Nisha. They were listening, but their attention was turned elsewhere. I could see her take his hand and place it over her growing belly. Around the normal café noises—scraping chairs and brewing coffee pots—I heard Kabir draw in a sharp gasp.

My eyes filled with happy tears and I wiped them away, turning my attention back to my audience. 'Love hard and forgive mistakes. Not only other people's mistakes, but your own as well.'

The crowd once again started applauding, and I smiled.

'What will you do now?' a girl from the corner table asked, her voice projecting to be heard.

Vivaan stood up as he made his way to the front to stand next to me. A ripple of applause rolled though the audience as they realized who Vivaan was.

He draped his arm over my shoulder possessively and squeezed it. 'We are going to travel the world together and continue to write stories about our journeys,' he said confidently.

'Where will you go?'

I spoke up. '*Anywhere and everywhere. But always together.*'

He dropped a kiss on my forehead before turning back to the audience. 'Although you have the book in your hands, our story is far from over.'

ACKNOWLEDGEMENTS

I would like to express my gratitude to many people who saw me through this book; to all those who provided support, talked things over, read, wrote, offered comments, remarks and assisted in making this book better.

I want to thank my parents, family and friends who supported and encouraged me in spite of all the time it took me away from them.

Most importantly, I want to thank my mentor, Ashish Bagrecha, for making me what I am today.

Finally, thanks to my publishers Westland Ltd., led by Gautam Padmanabhan, for realizing my potential and helping me tell my stories.